ANN M. MARTIN
BABY-SITTERS LITTLE SISTER®

KAREN'S ROLLER SKATES

A GRAPHIC NOVEL BY
KATY FARINA
WITH COLOR BY BRADEN LAMB

graphix

An Imprint of
SCHOLASTIC

This book is in loving memory
of my grandmother Adele Read Martin
August 2, 1894 – April 18, 1988
A. M. M.

For my parents, who were always there to
make scrapes, sickness, and broken bones feel better
K. F.

Text copyright © 2020 by Ann M. Martin
Art copyright © 2020 by Katy Farina

Library of Congress Control Number: 2019945281

ISBN 978-1-338-35616-8 (hardcover)
ISBN 978-1-338-35614-4 (paperback)

10 9 8 7 6 5 4 3 2   20 21 22 23 24

Printed in Malaysia   108
First edition, July 2020

Edited by Cassandra Pelham Fulton and David Levithan
Book design by Phil Falco and Shivana Sookdeo
Penciling assistance from Kendra Wells
Publisher: David Saylor

CHAPTER 1

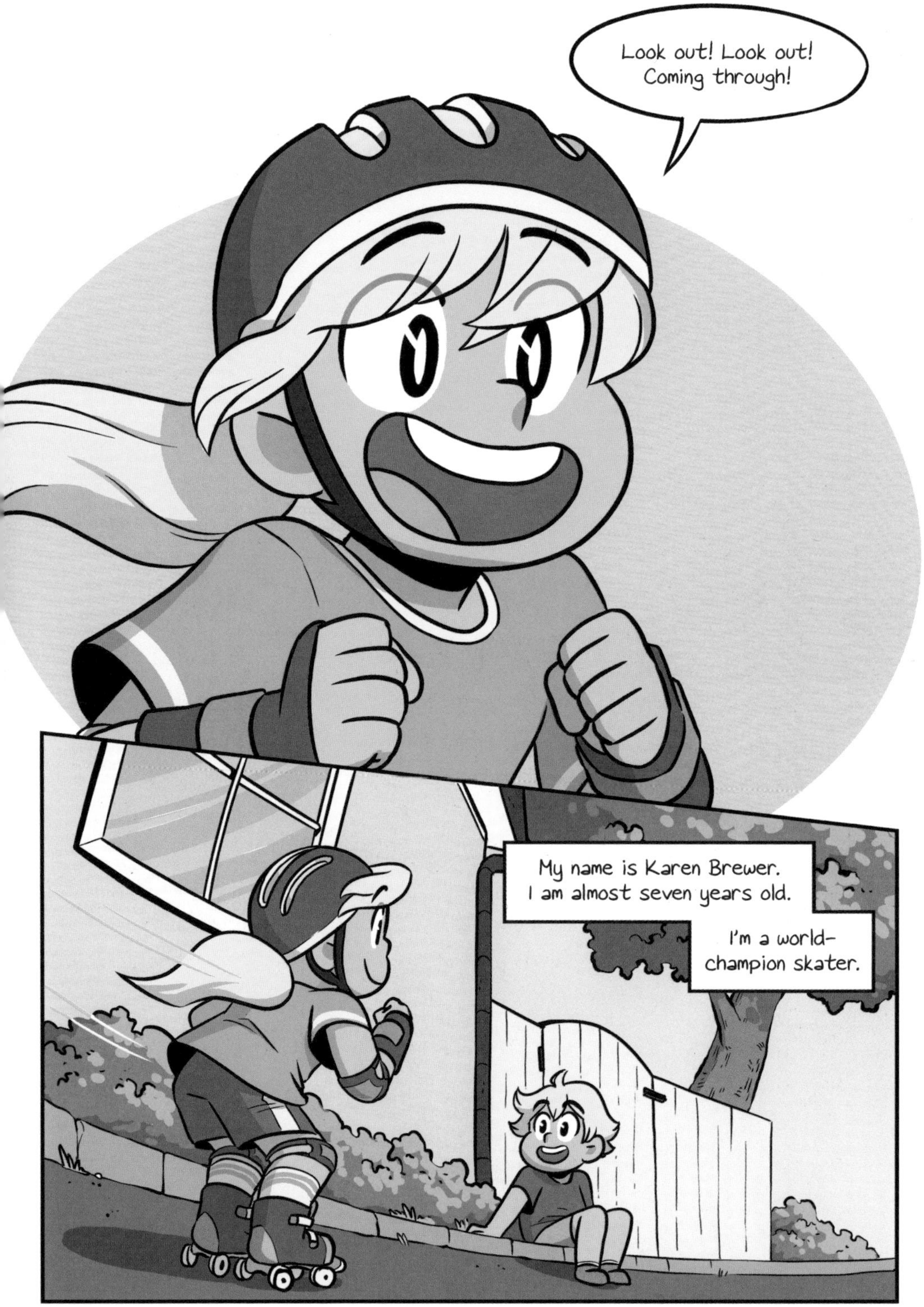
Look out! Look out! Coming through!
My name is Karen Brewer. I am almost seven years old.
I'm a world-champion skater.

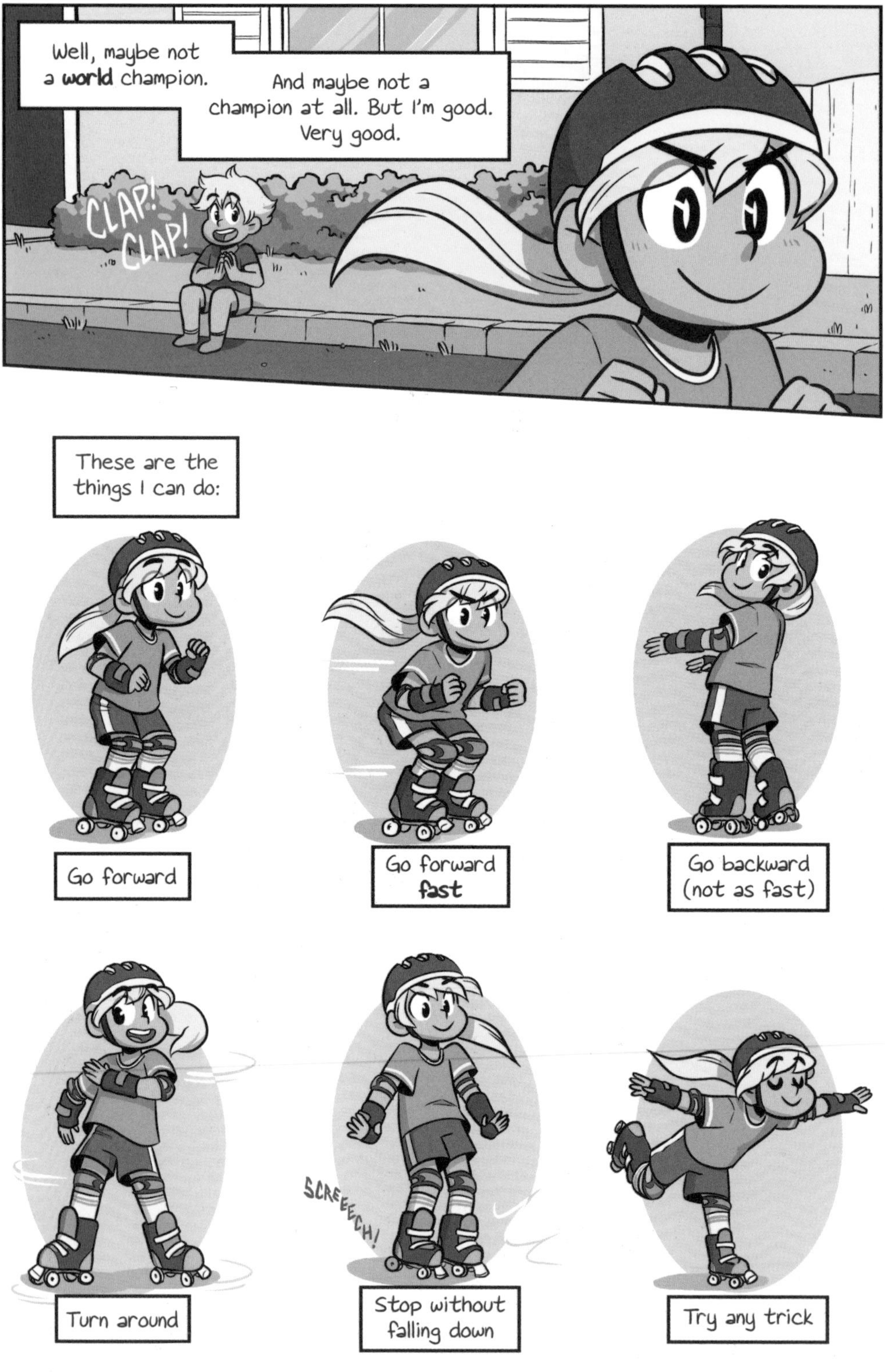
Well, maybe not a **world** champion.
And maybe not a champion at all. But I'm good. Very good.
CLAP! CLAP!
These are the things I can do:
Go forward
Go forward **fast**
Go backward (not as fast)
Turn around
SCREEECH!
Stop without falling down
Try any trick

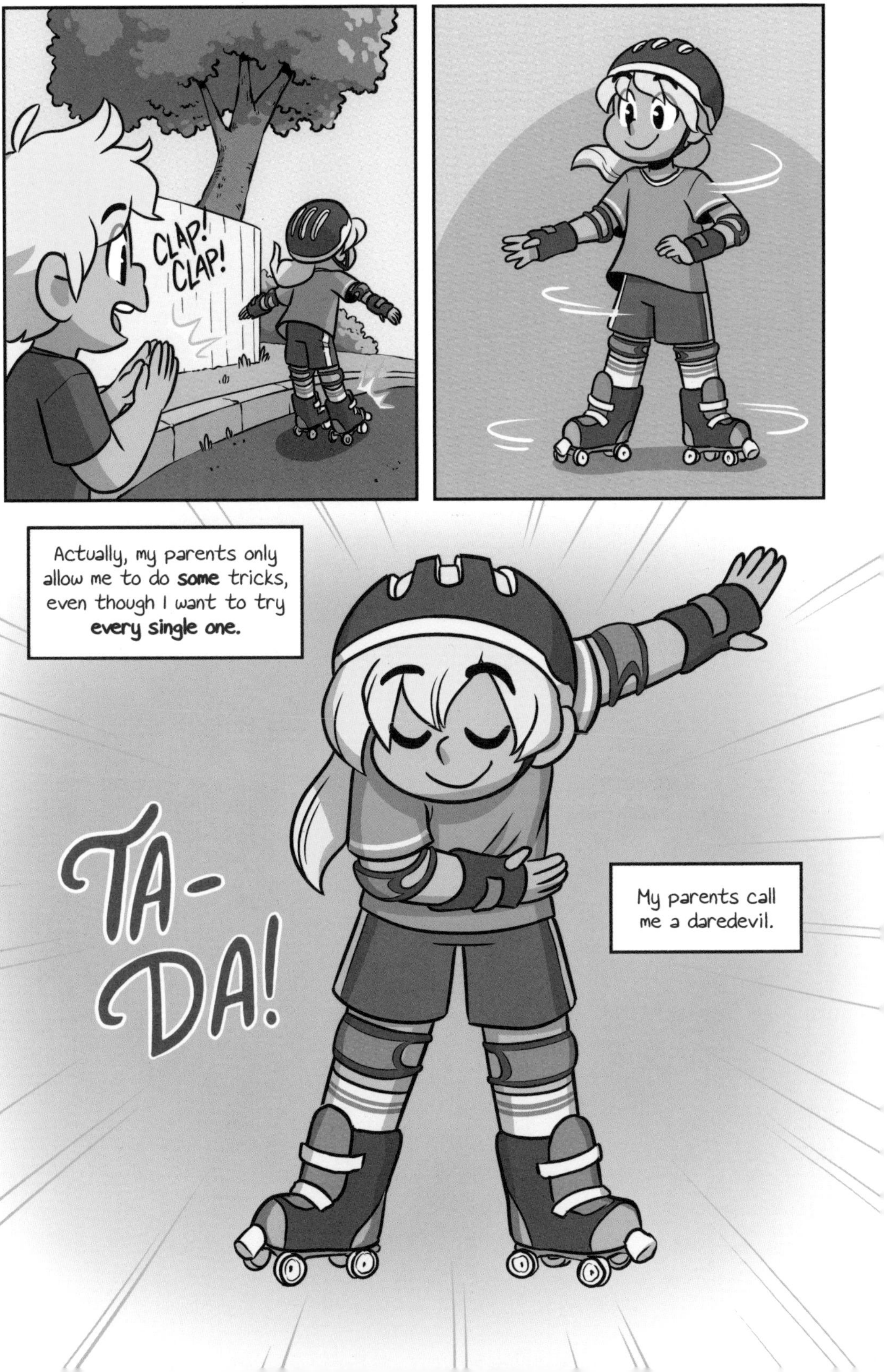
CLAP! CLAP!
Actually, my parents only allow me to do **some** tricks, even though I want to try **every single one.**
TA-DA!
My parents call me a daredevil.

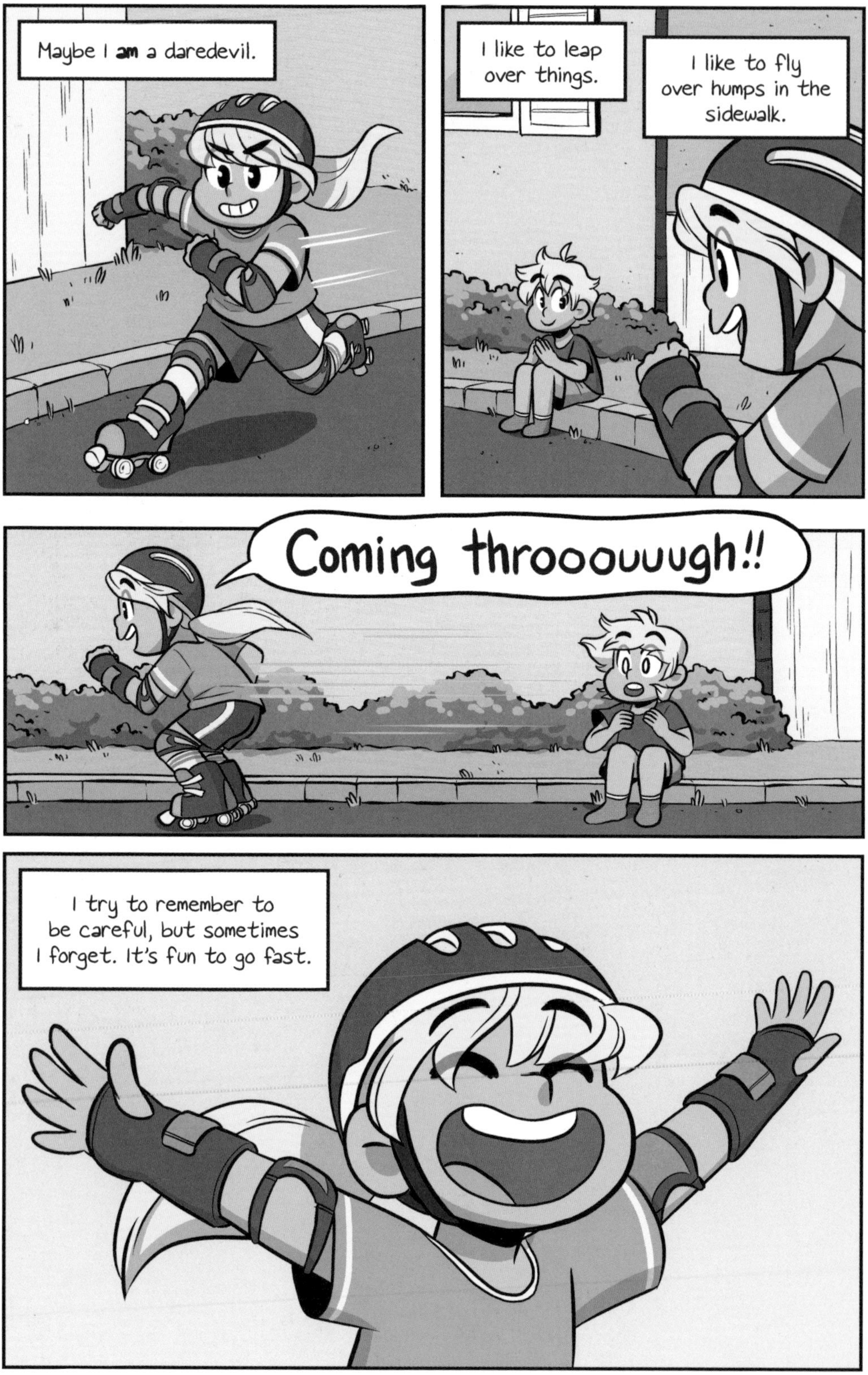

Maybe I **am** a daredevil.
I like to leap over things.
I like to fly over humps in the sidewalk.
Coming throooouuugh!!
I try to remember to be careful, but sometimes I forget. It's fun to go fast.

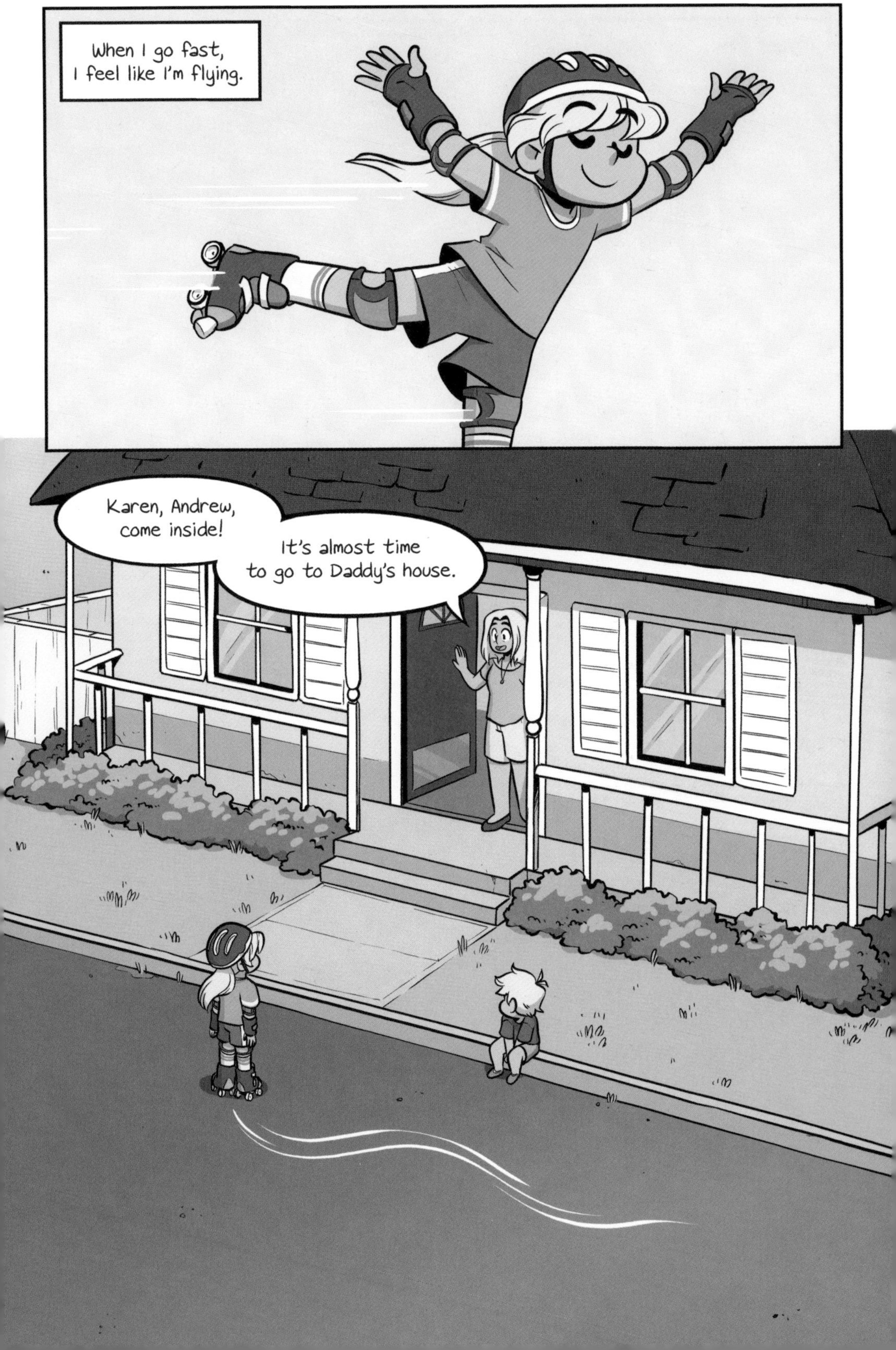
When I go fast, I feel like I'm flying.
Karen, Andrew, come inside!
It's almost time to go to Daddy's house.

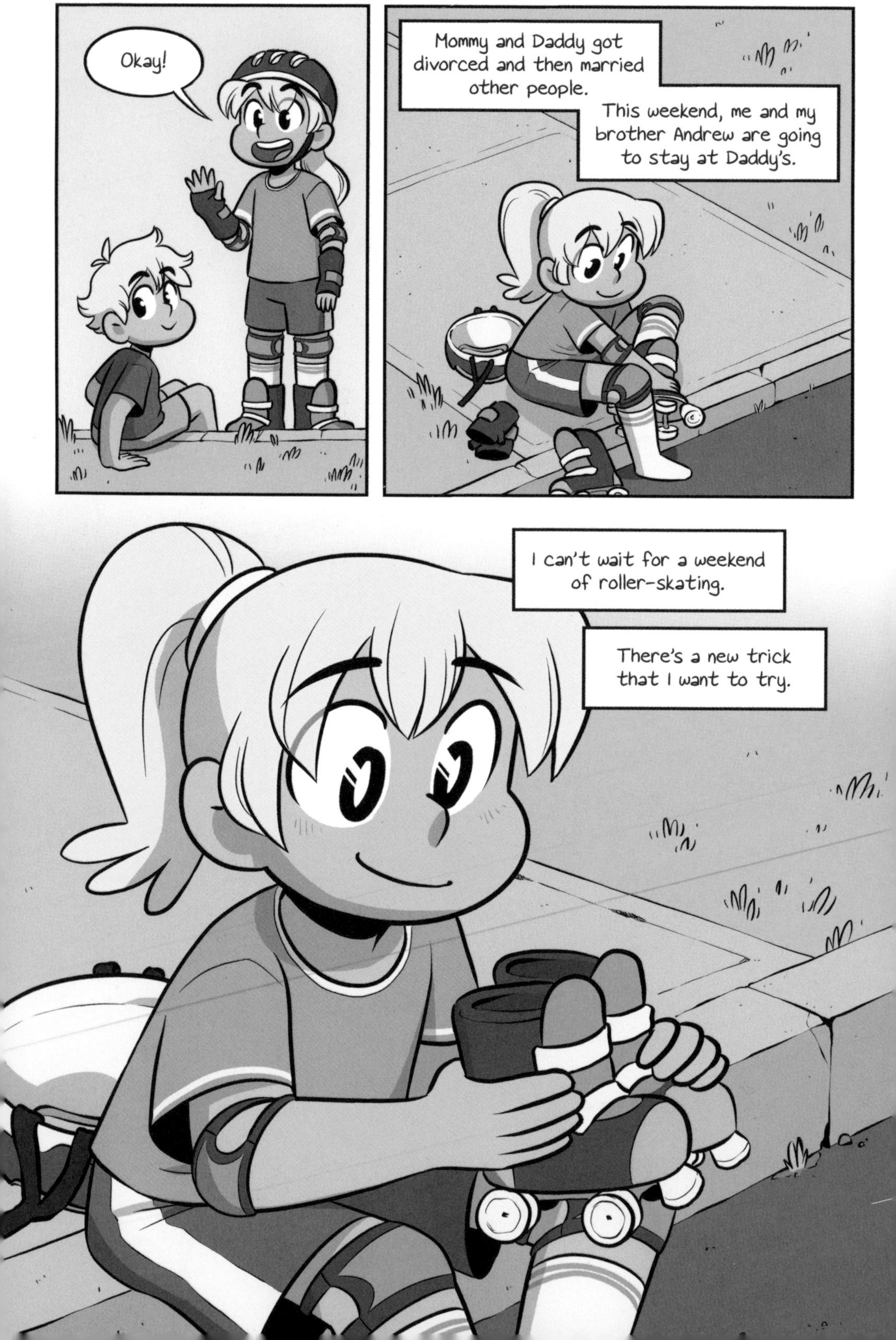
Okay!
Mommy and Daddy got divorced and then married other people.
This weekend, me and my brother Andrew are going to stay at Daddy's.
I can't wait for a weekend of roller-skating.
There's a new trick that I want to try.

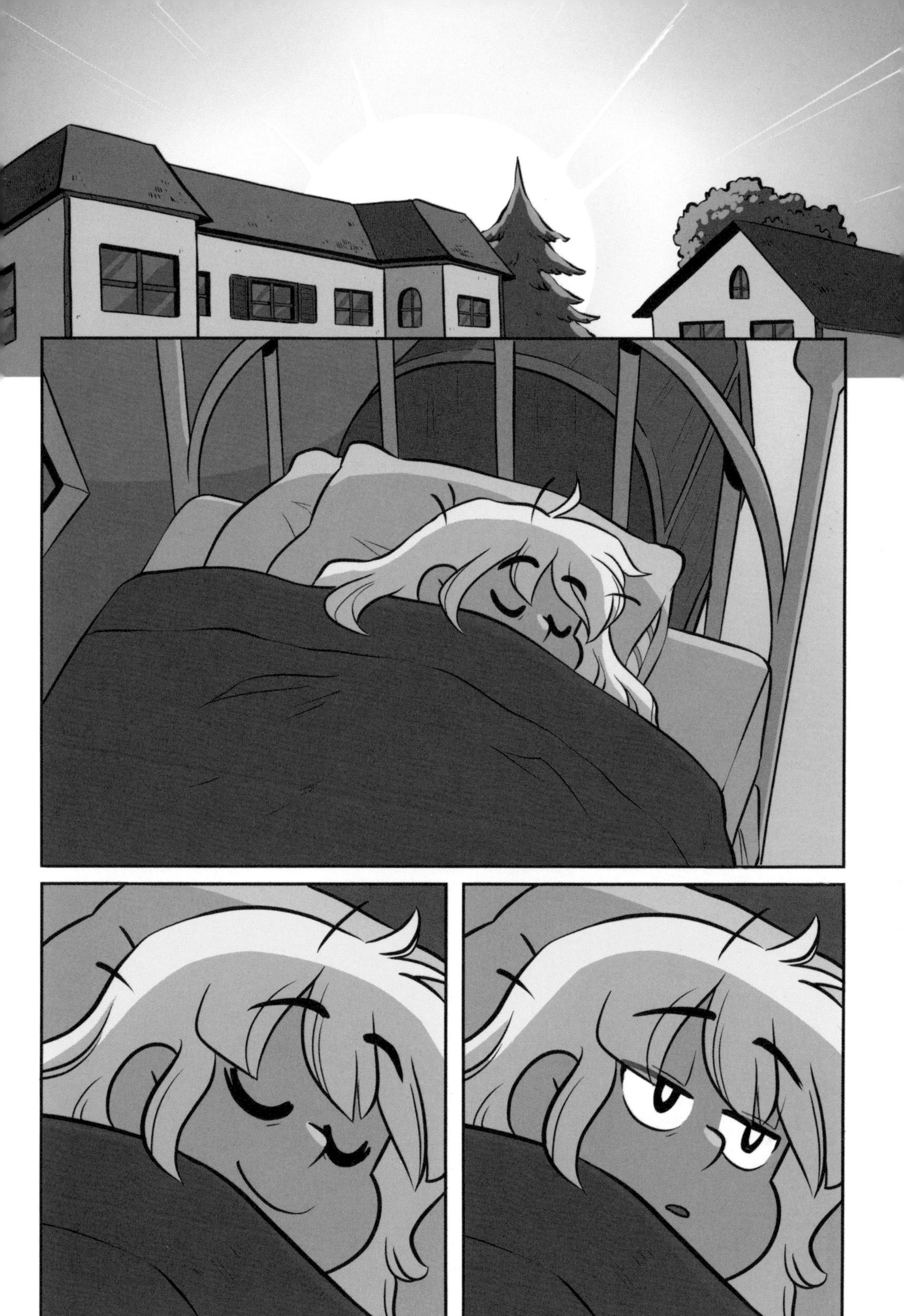

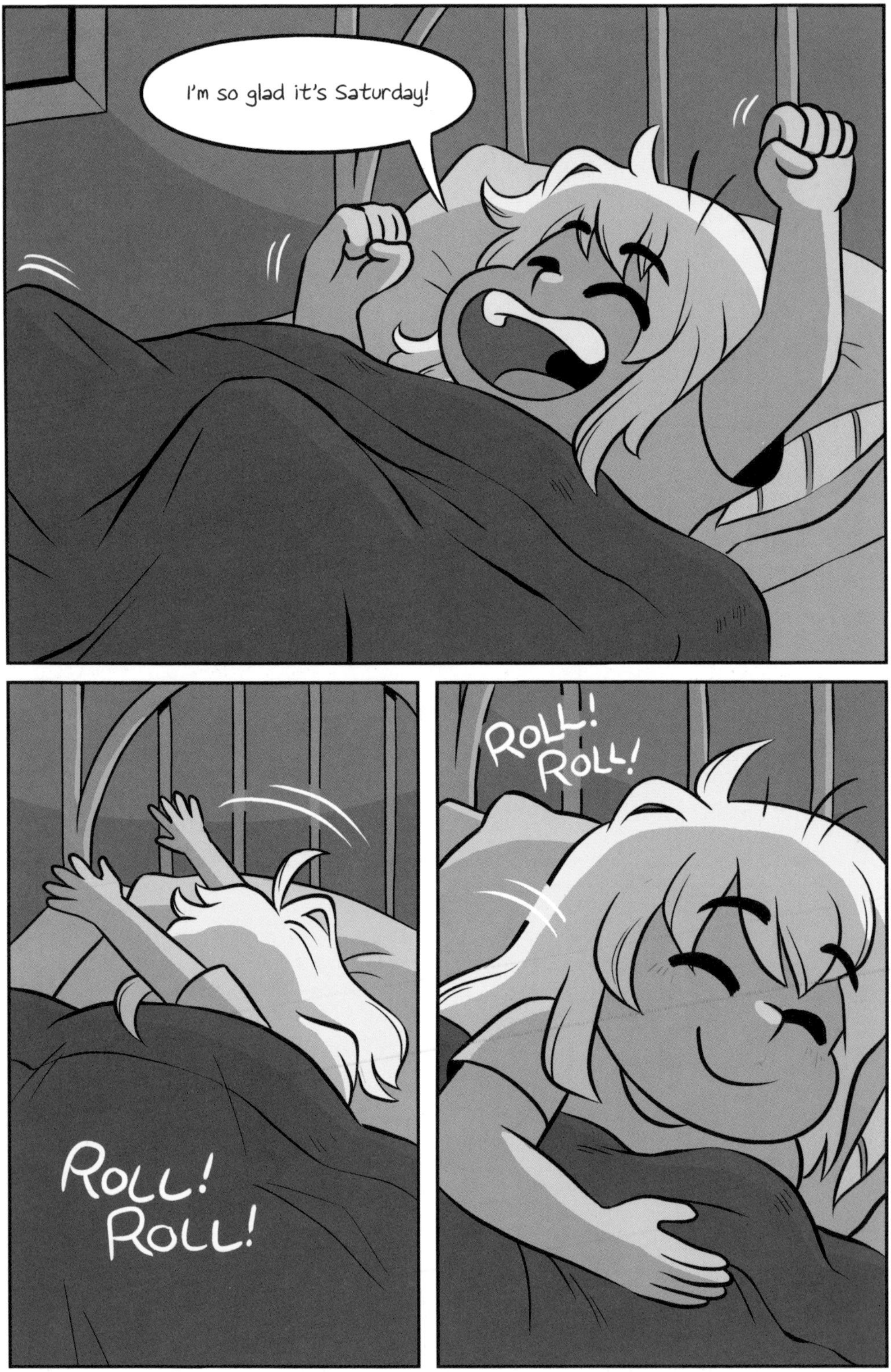
I'm so glad it's Saturday!
ROLL! ROLL!
ROLL! ROLL!

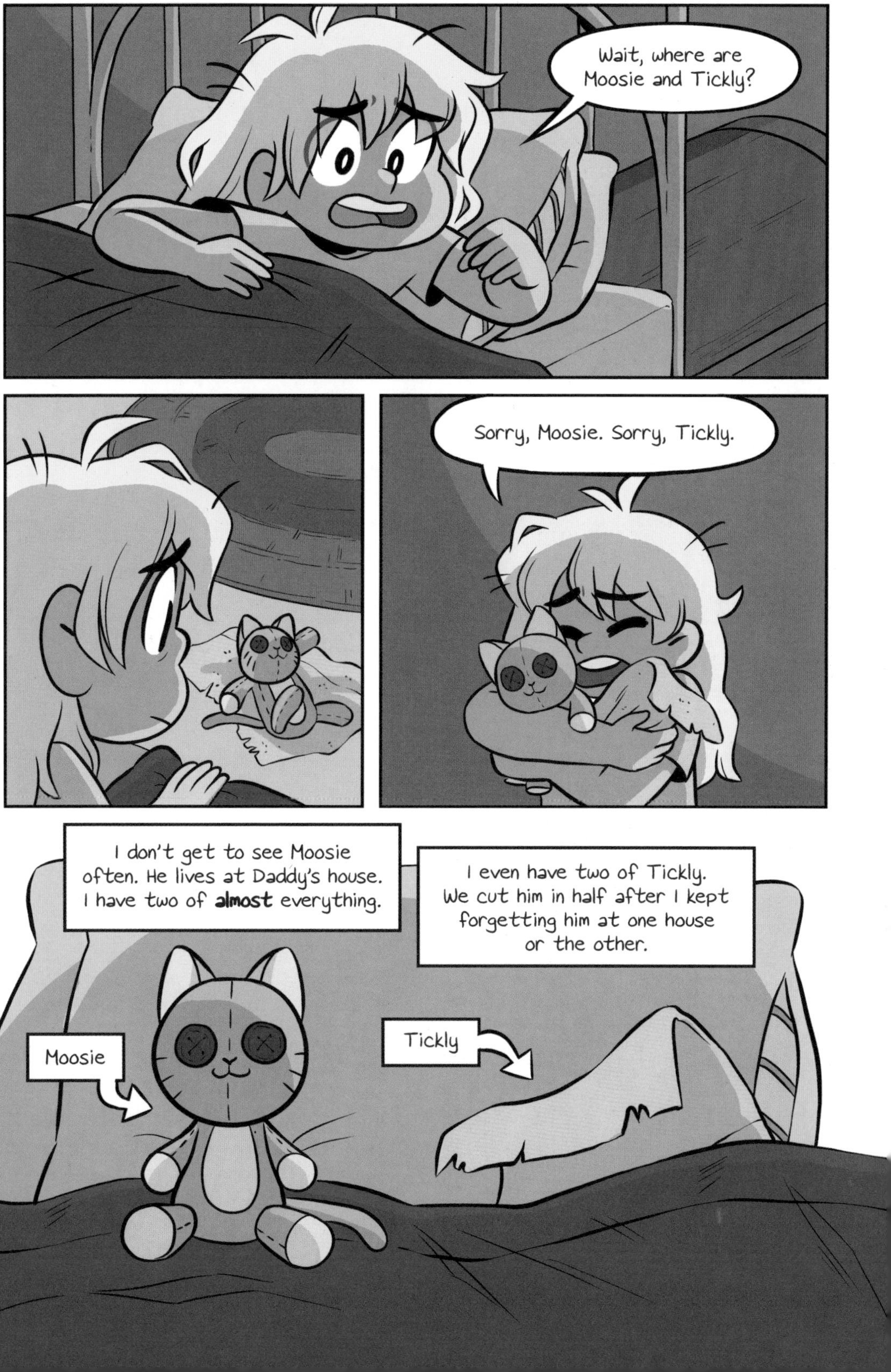
Wait, where are Moosie and Tickly?
Sorry, Moosie. Sorry, Tickly.
I don't get to see Moosie often. He lives at Daddy's house. I have two of **almost** everything.
I even have two of Tickly. We cut him in half after I kept forgetting him at one house or the other.
Moosie
Tickly

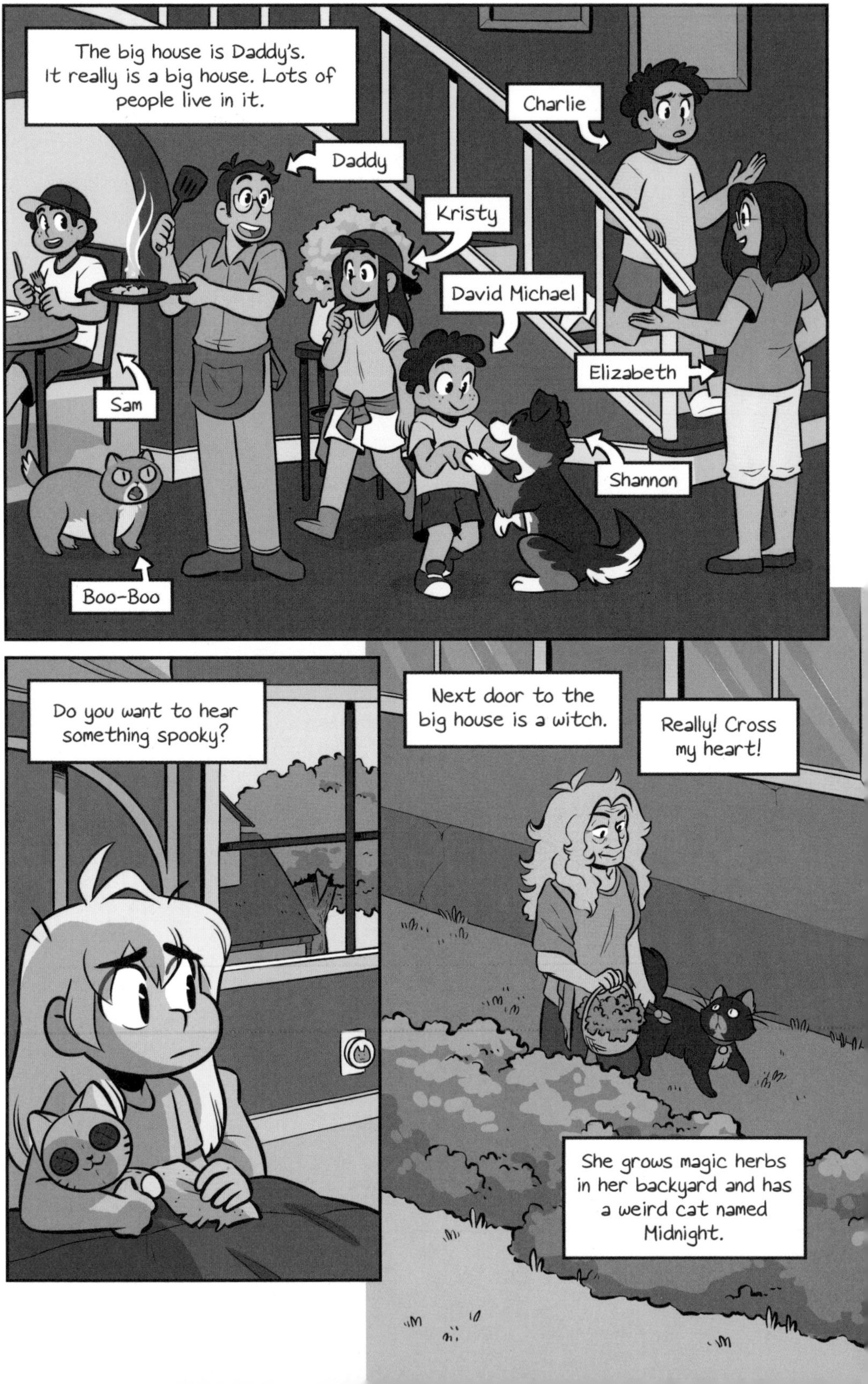
The big house is Daddy's.
It really is a big house. Lots of people live in it.
Charlie
Daddy
Kristy
David Michael
Elizabeth
Sam
Shannon
Boo-Boo
Do you want to hear something spooky?
Next door to the big house is a witch.
Really! Cross my heart!
She grows magic herbs in her backyard and has a weird cat named Midnight.

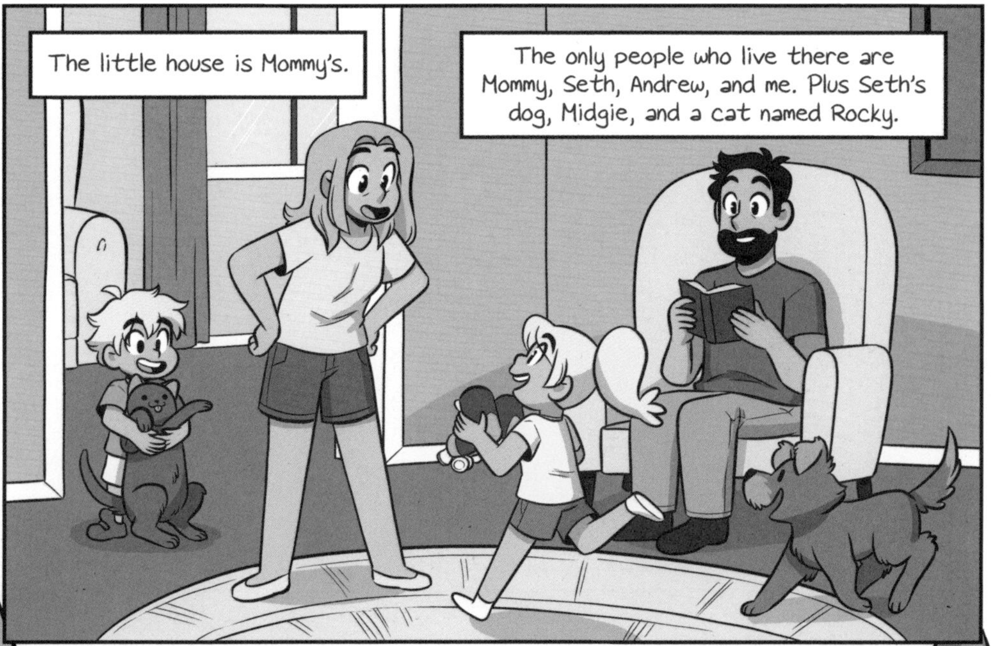
The little house is Mommy's.
The only people who live there are Mommy, Seth, Andrew, and me. Plus Seth's dog, Midgie, and a cat named Rocky.

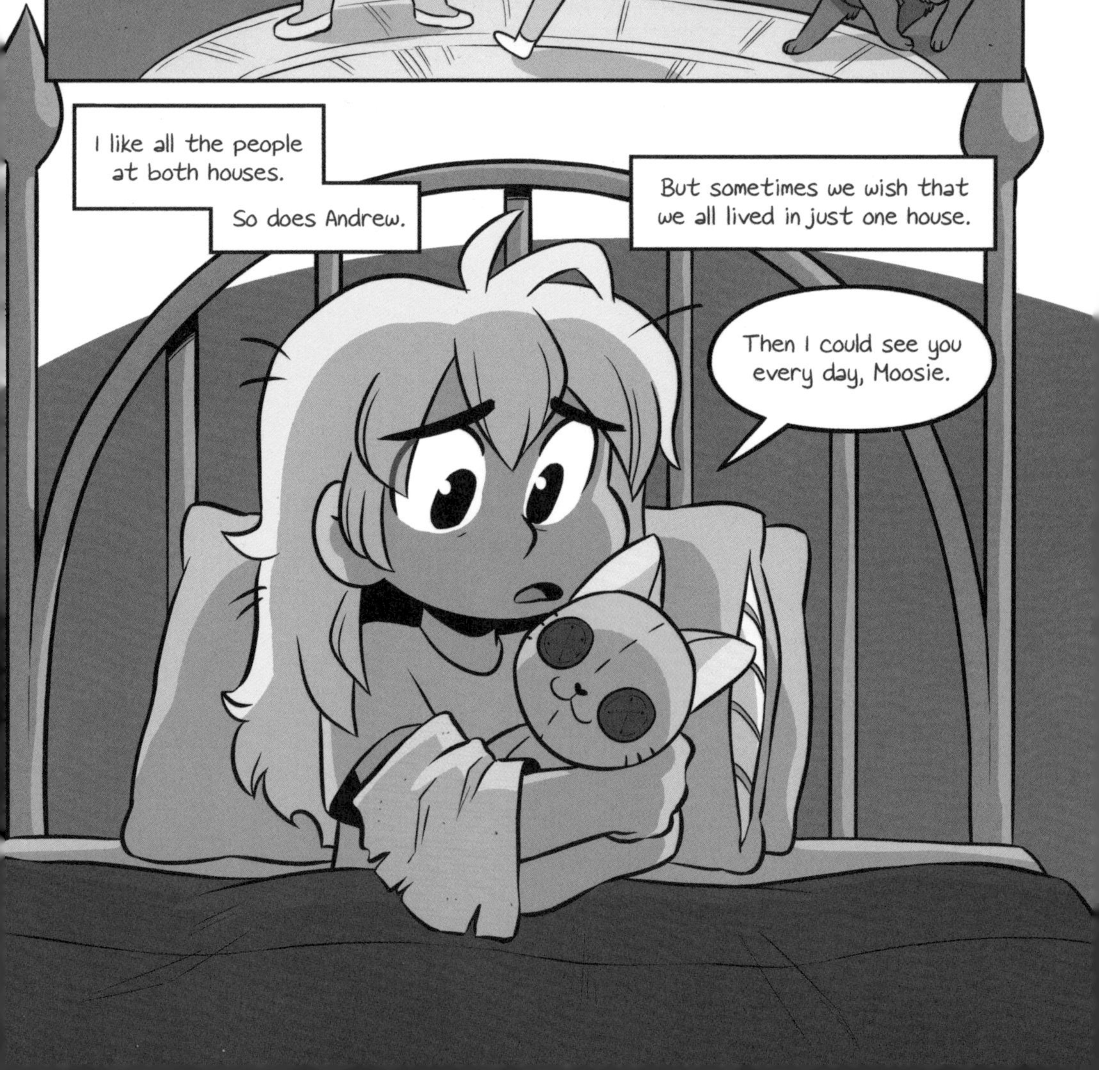
I like all the people at both houses.
So does Andrew.
But sometimes we wish that we all lived in just one house.
Then I could see you every day, Moosie.

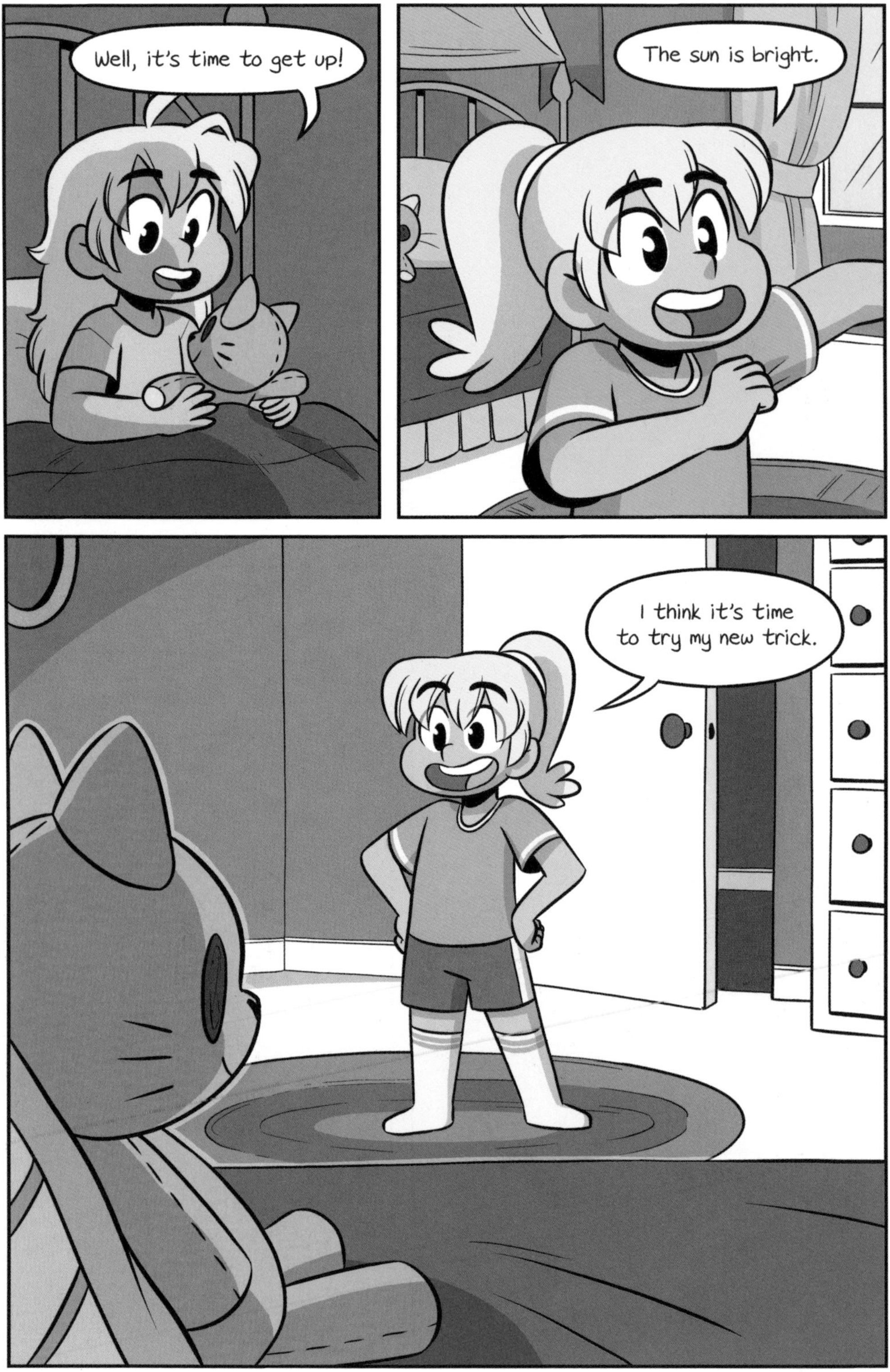
Well, it's time to get up!
The sun is bright.
I think it's time to try my new trick.

CHAPTER 2

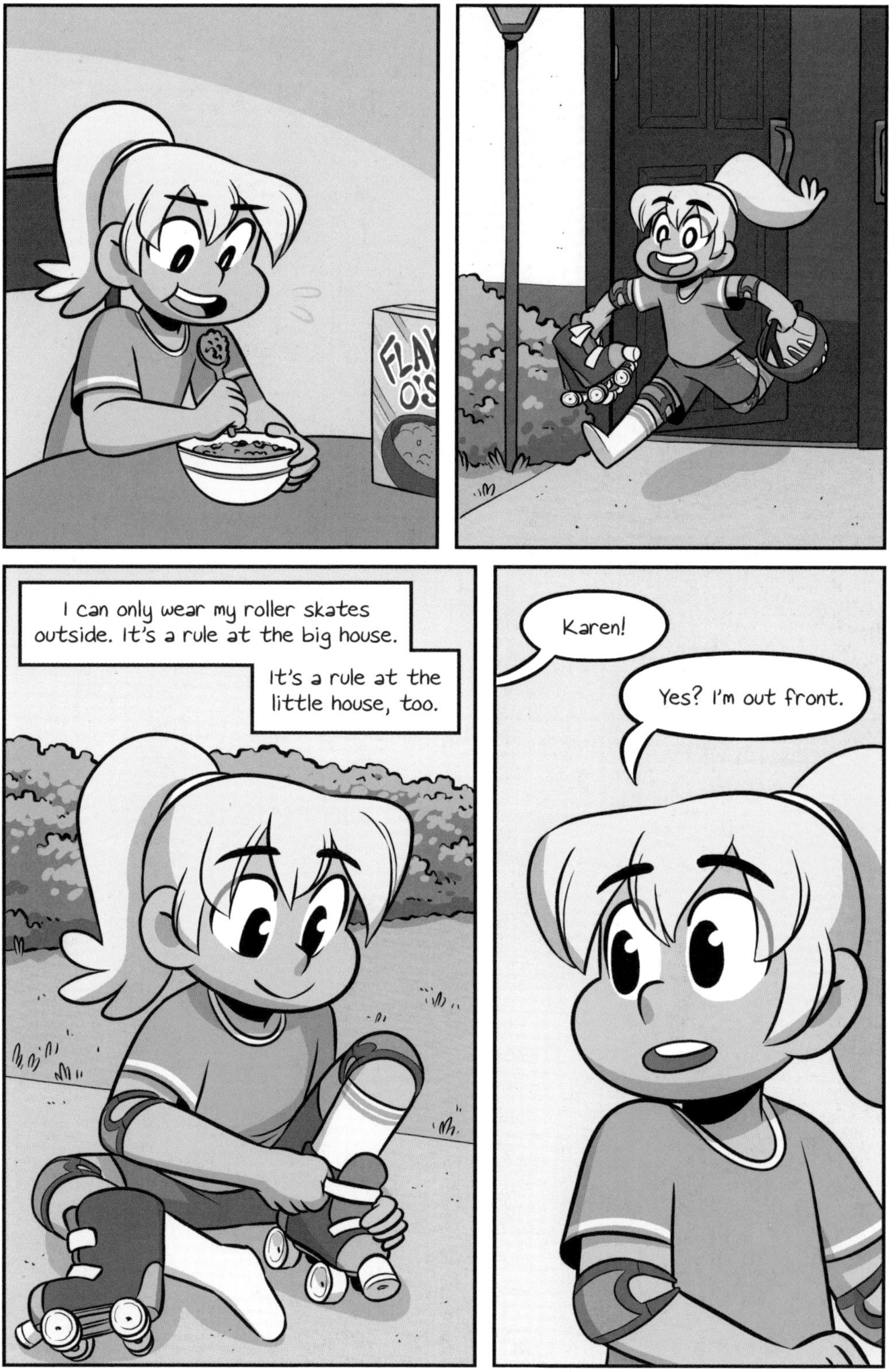
FLAK O'S
I can only wear my roller skates outside. It's a rule at the big house.
It's a rule at the little house, too.
Karen!
Yes? I'm out front.

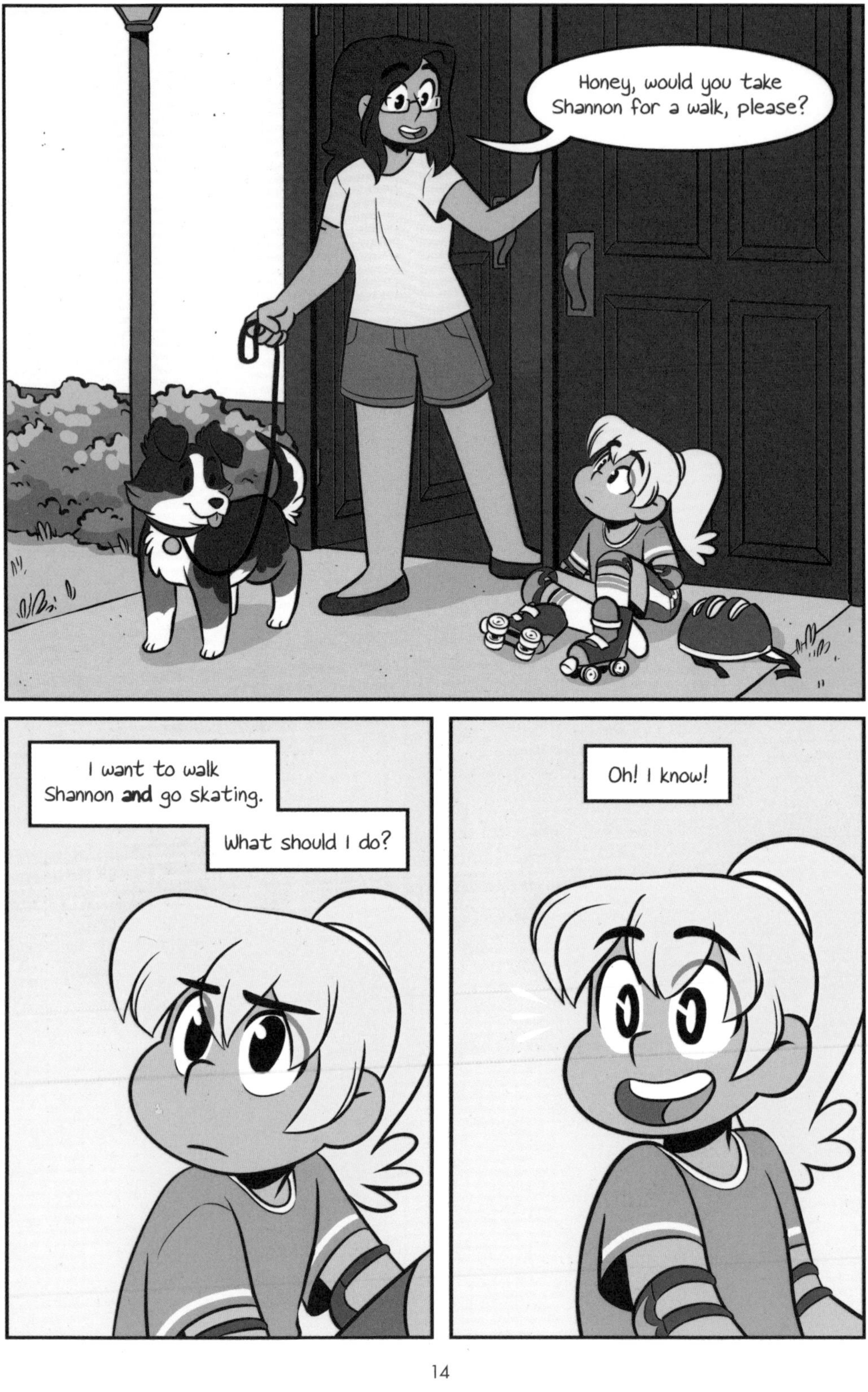
Honey, would you take Shannon for a walk, please?
I want to walk Shannon and go skating.
What should I do?
Oh! I know!

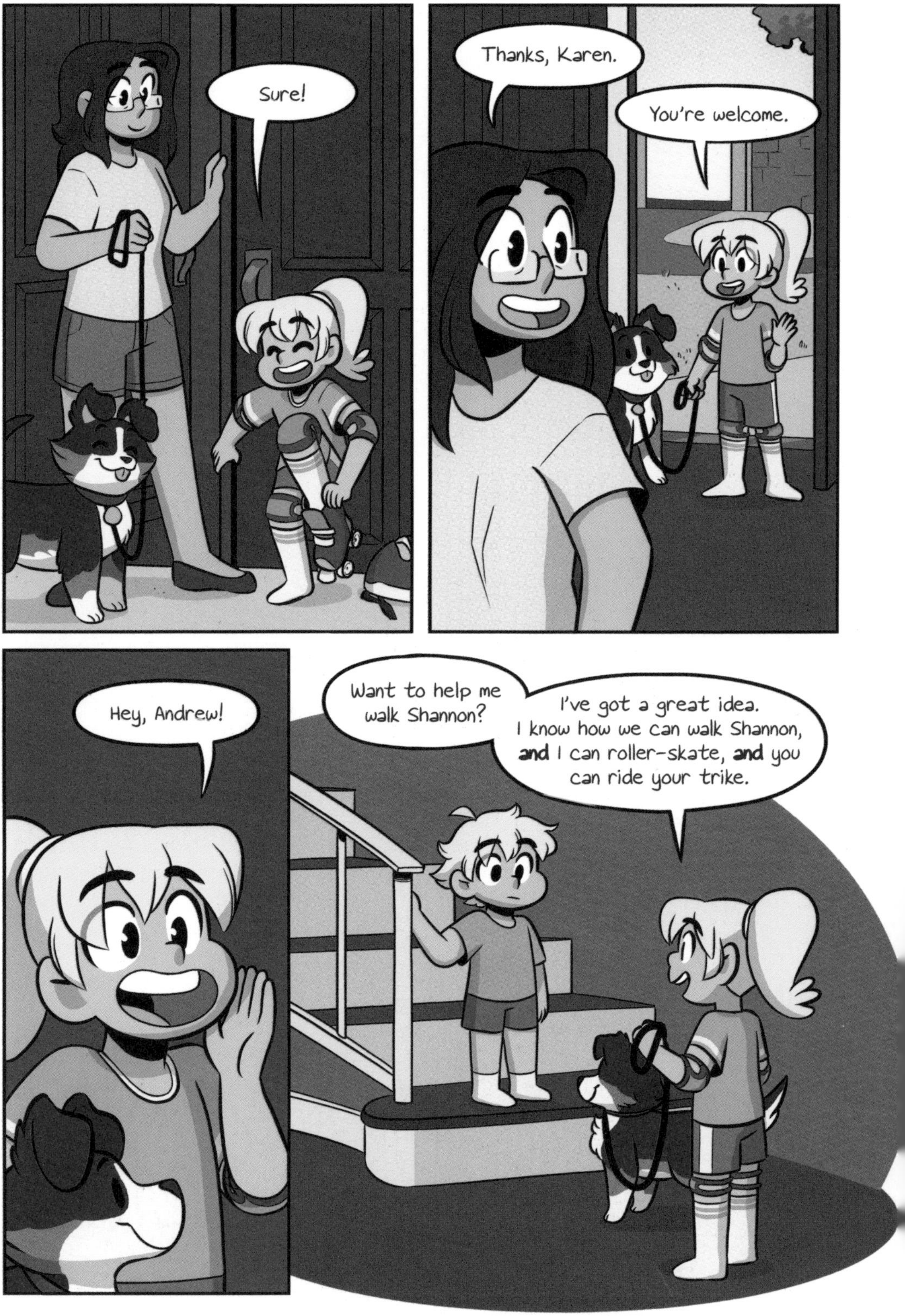
Sure!
Thanks, Karen.
You're welcome.
Hey, Andrew!
Want to help me walk Shannon?
I've got a great idea. I know how we can walk Shannon, **and** I can roller-skate, **and** you can ride your trike.

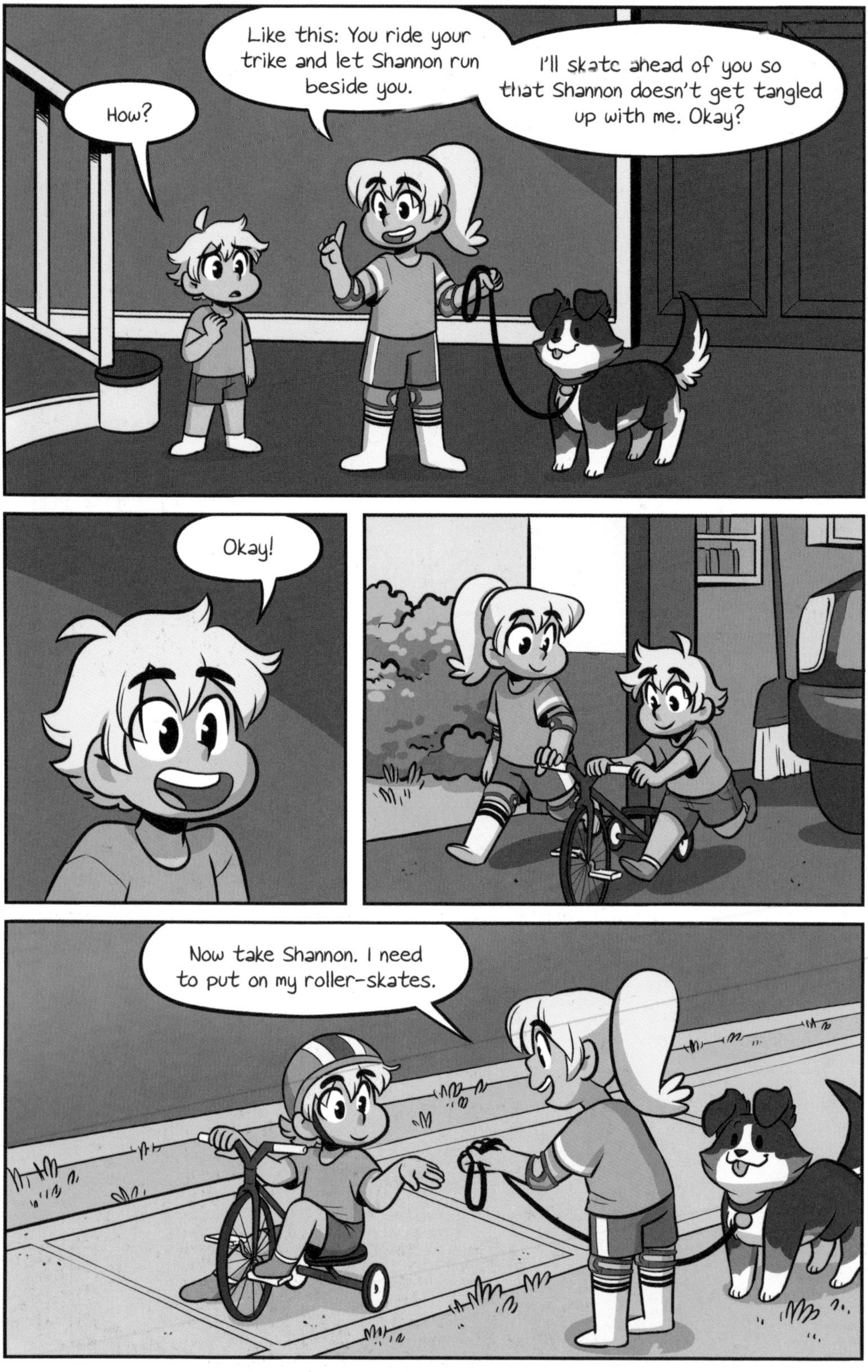
How?
Like this: You ride your trike and let Shannon run beside you.
I'll skate ahead of you so that Shannon doesn't get tangled up with me. Okay?
Okay!
Now take Shannon. I need to put on my roller-skates.

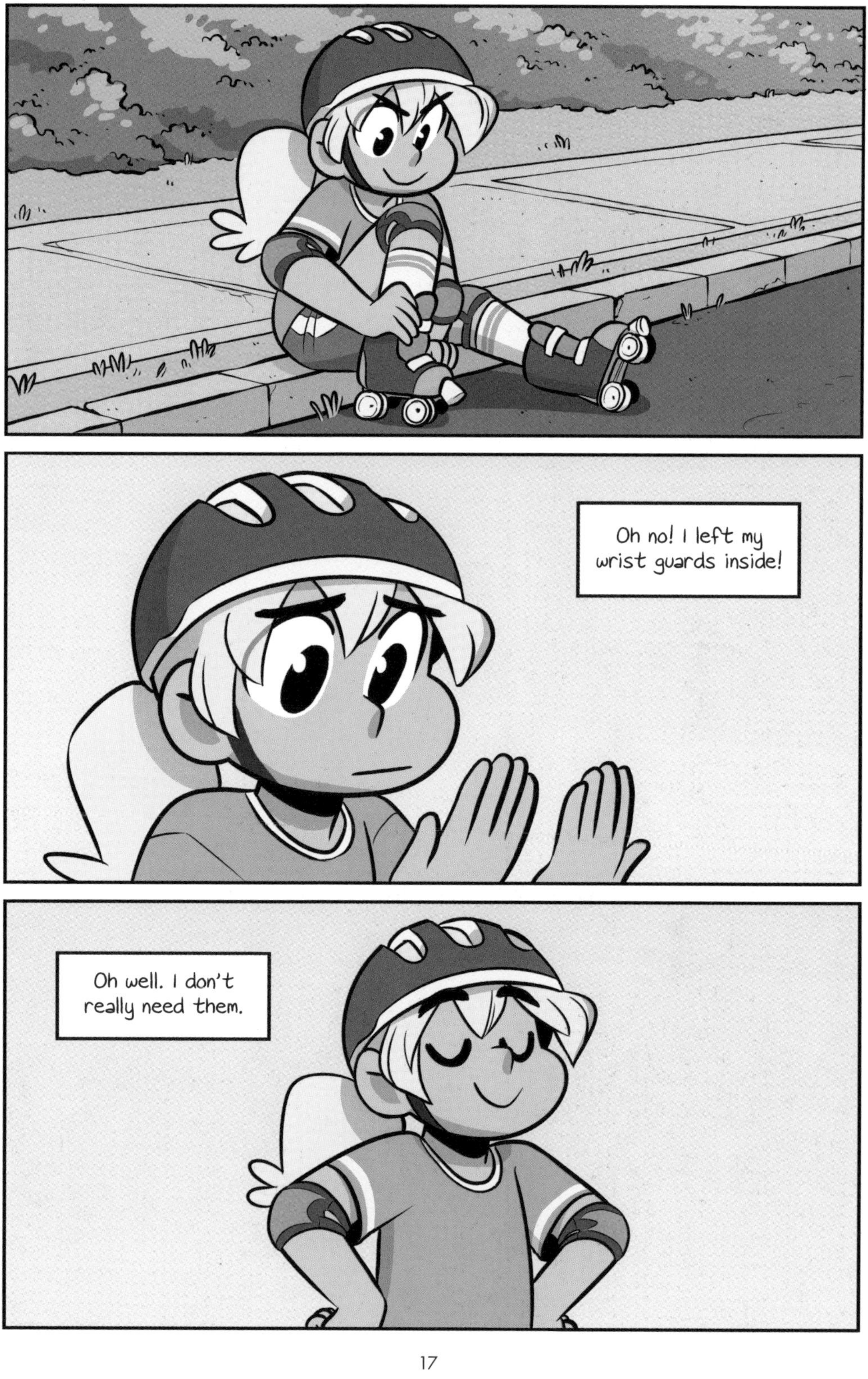
Oh no! I left my wrist guards inside!
Oh well. I don't really need them.

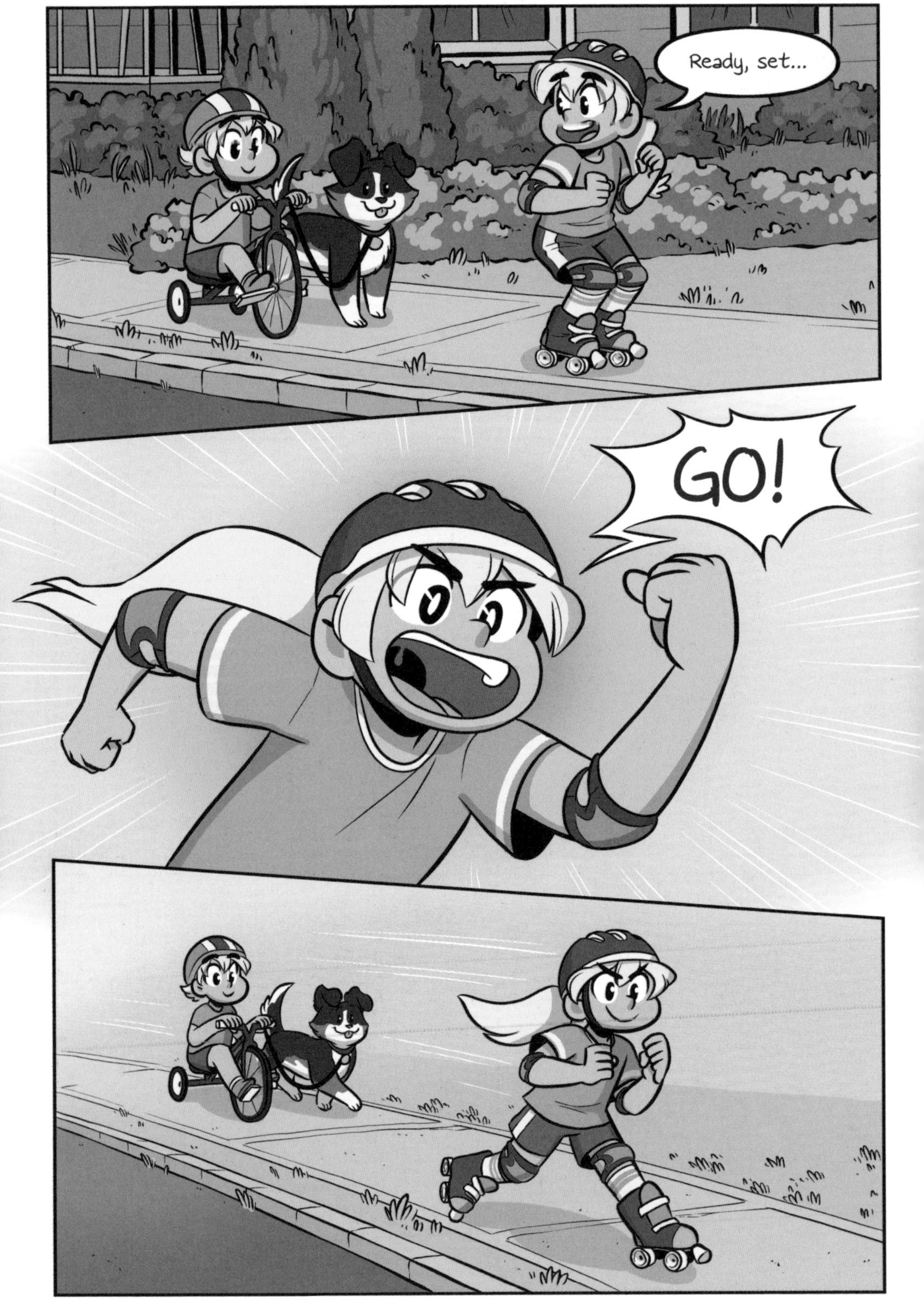
Ready, set...
GO!

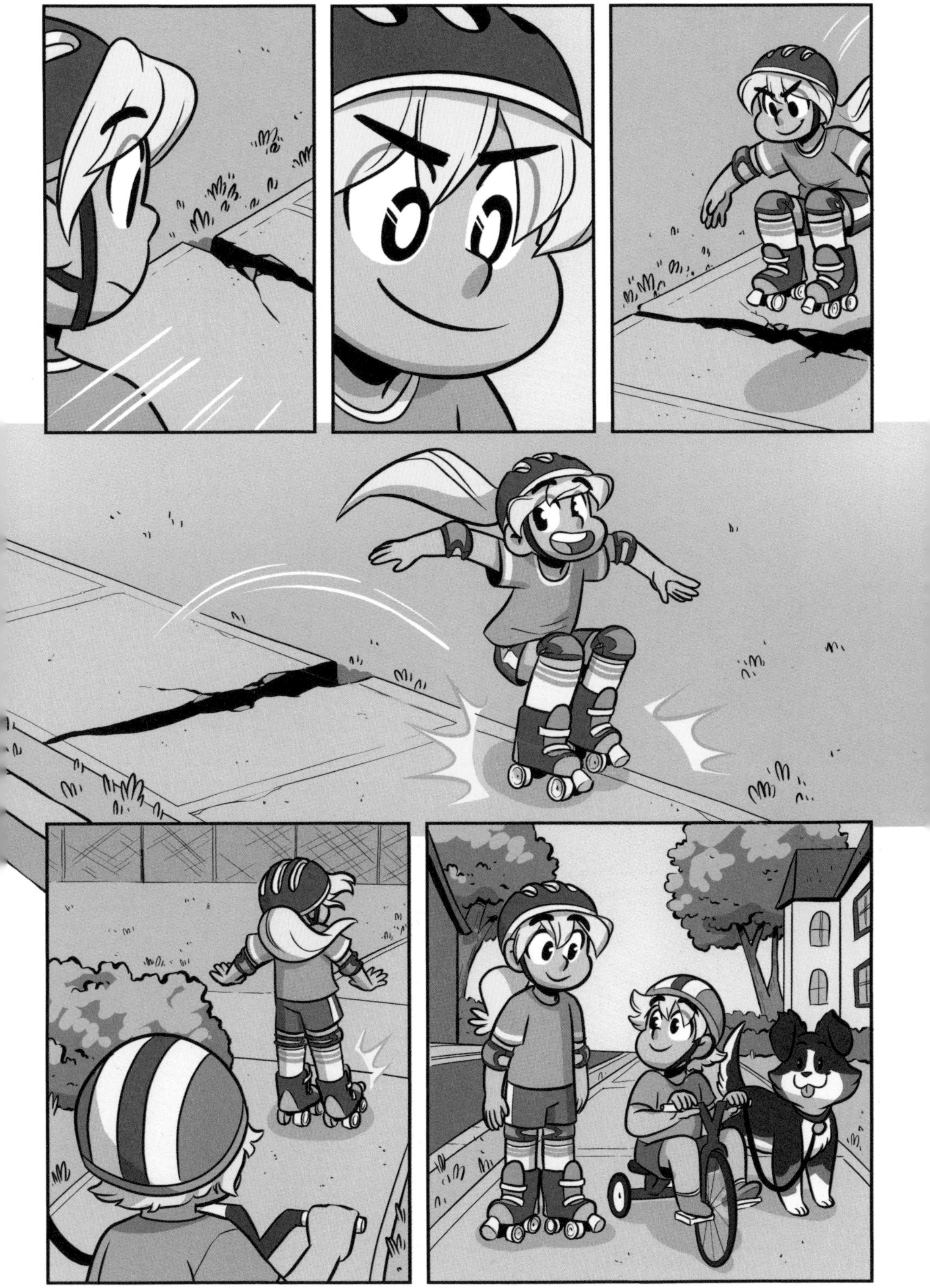

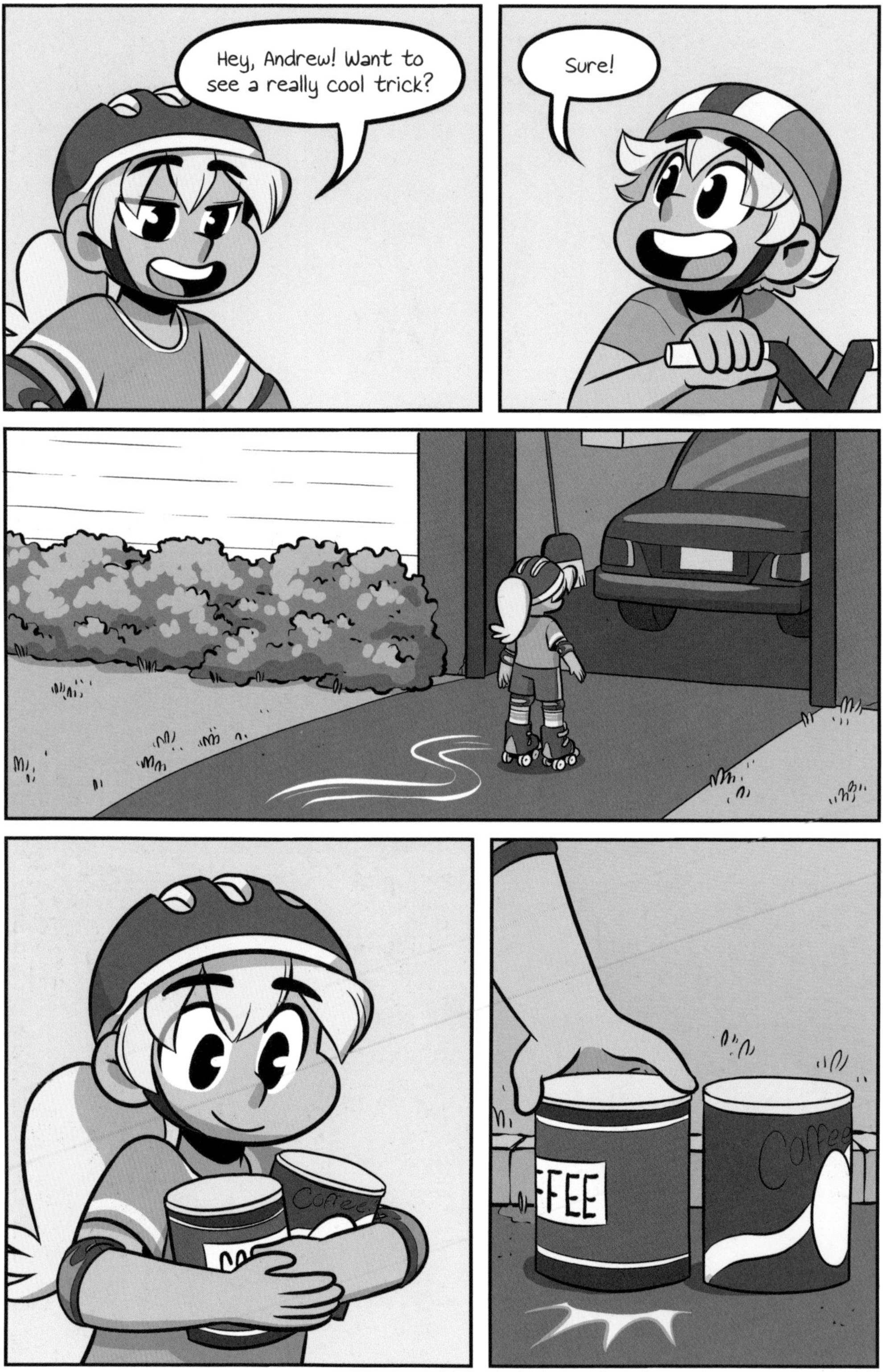
Hey, Andrew! Want to see a really cool trick?
Sure!
Coffee
FFEE
Coffee

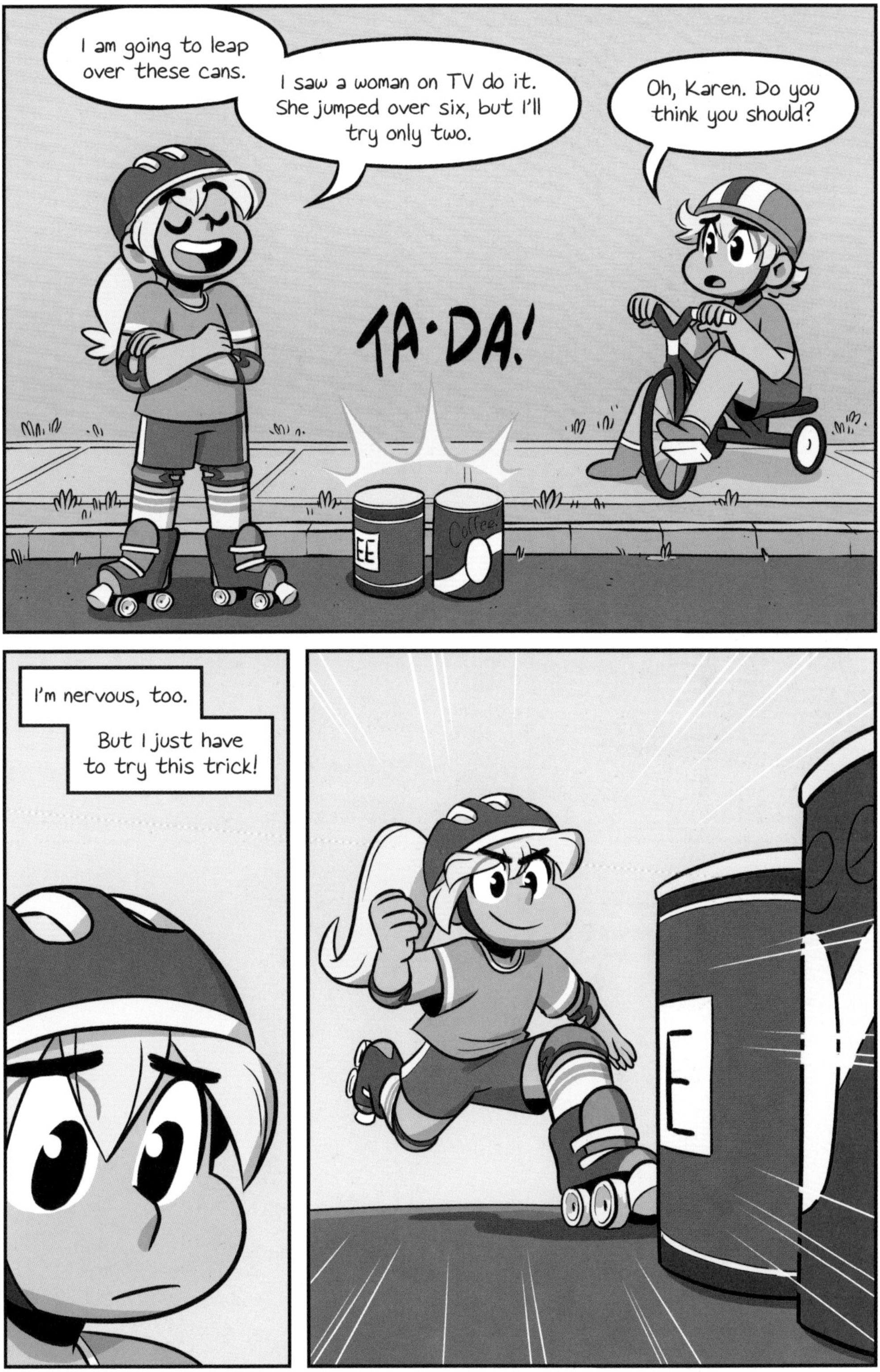
I am going to leap over these cans.
I saw a woman on TV do it. She jumped over six, but I'll try only two.
Oh, Karen. Do you think you should?
TA-DA!
I'm nervous, too.
But I just have to try this trick!

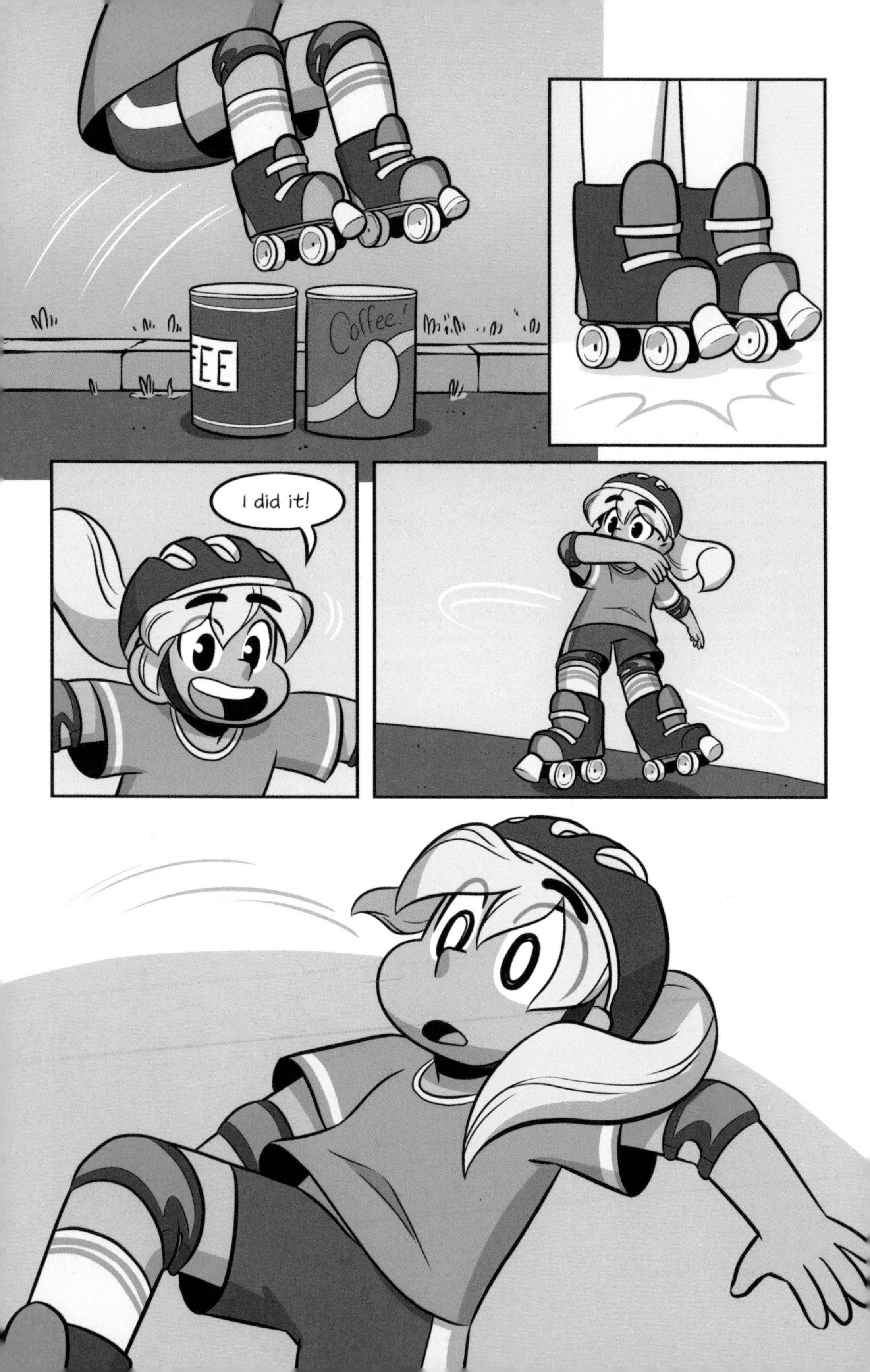
FEE
Coffee!
I did it!

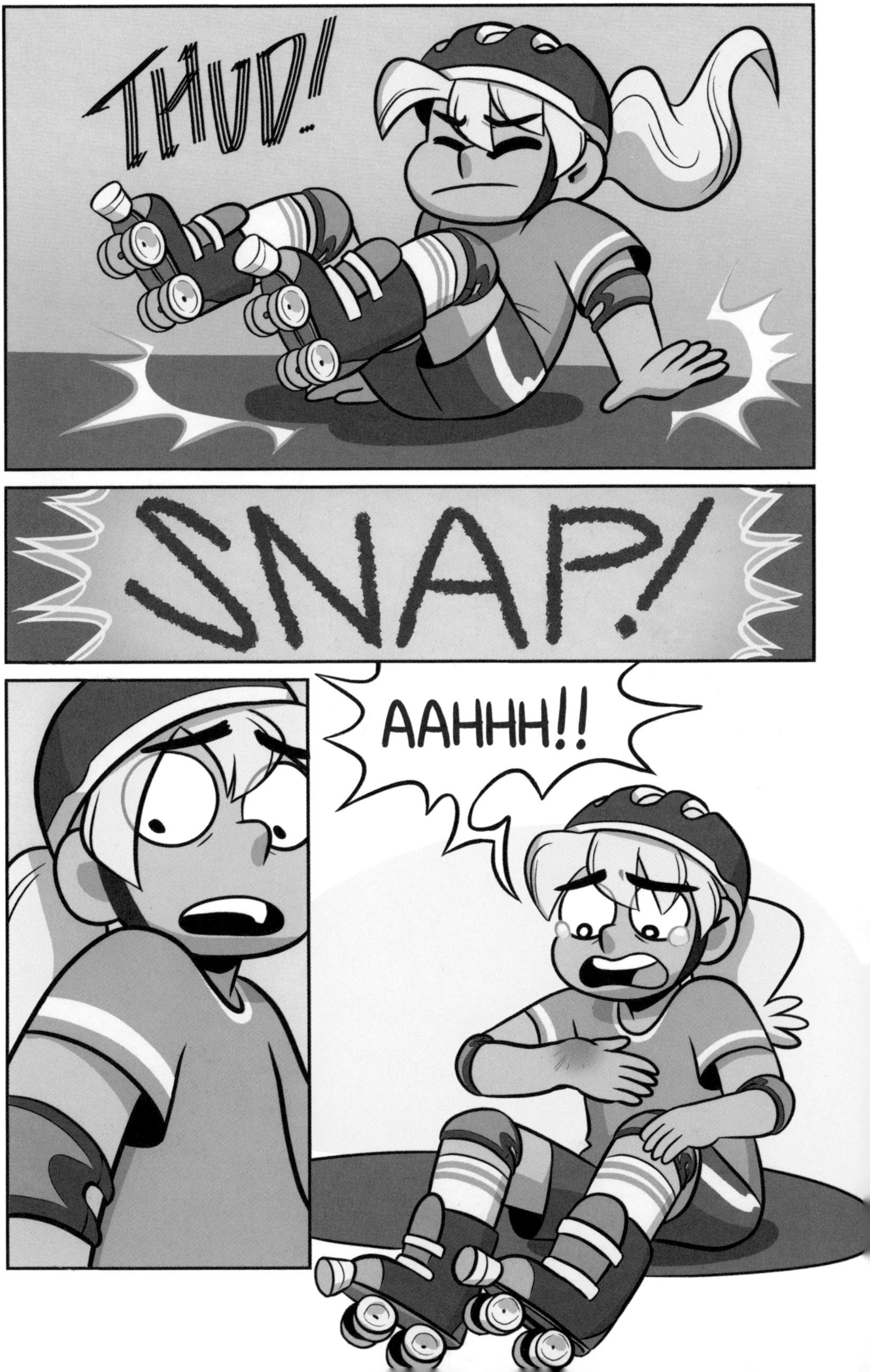
THUD!...
SNAP!
AAHHH!!

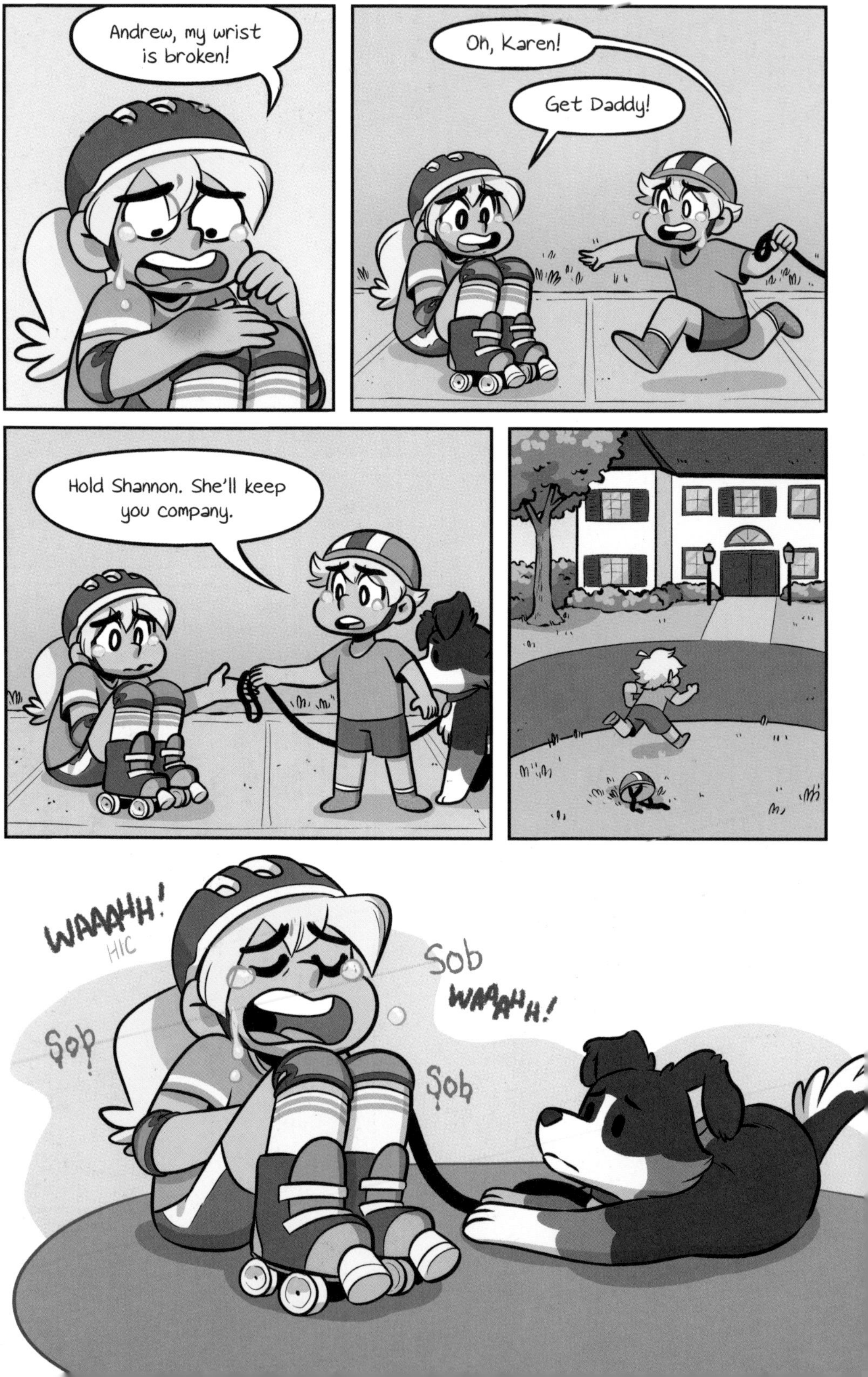
Andrew, my wrist is broken!
Oh, Karen!
Get Daddy!
Hold Shannon. She'll keep you company.
WAAAHH!
HIC
Sob
WAAAHH!
Sob
Sob

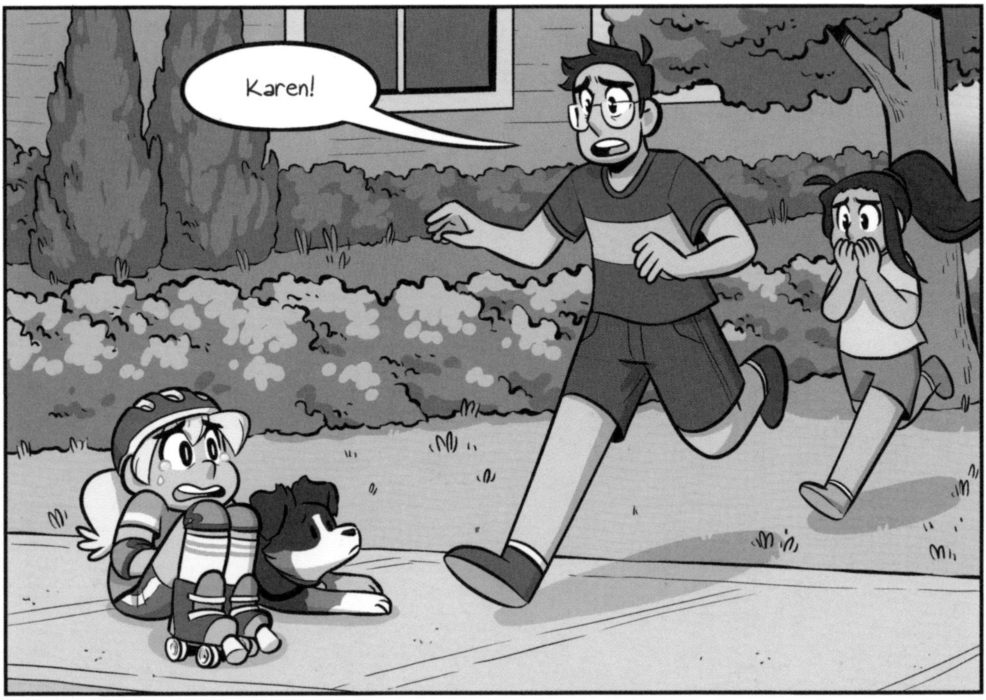
Karen!

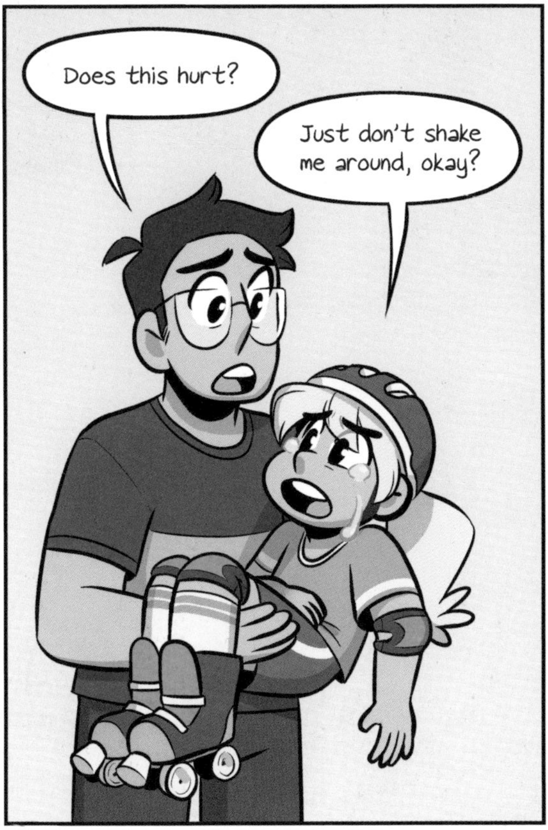
Does this hurt?
Just don't shake me around, okay?

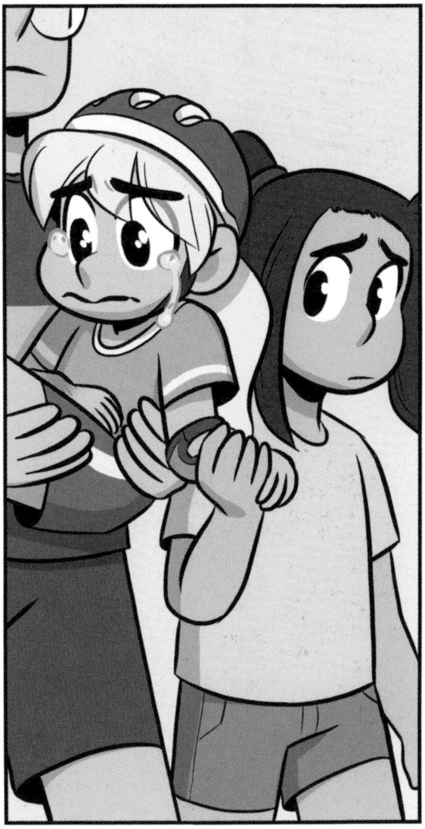

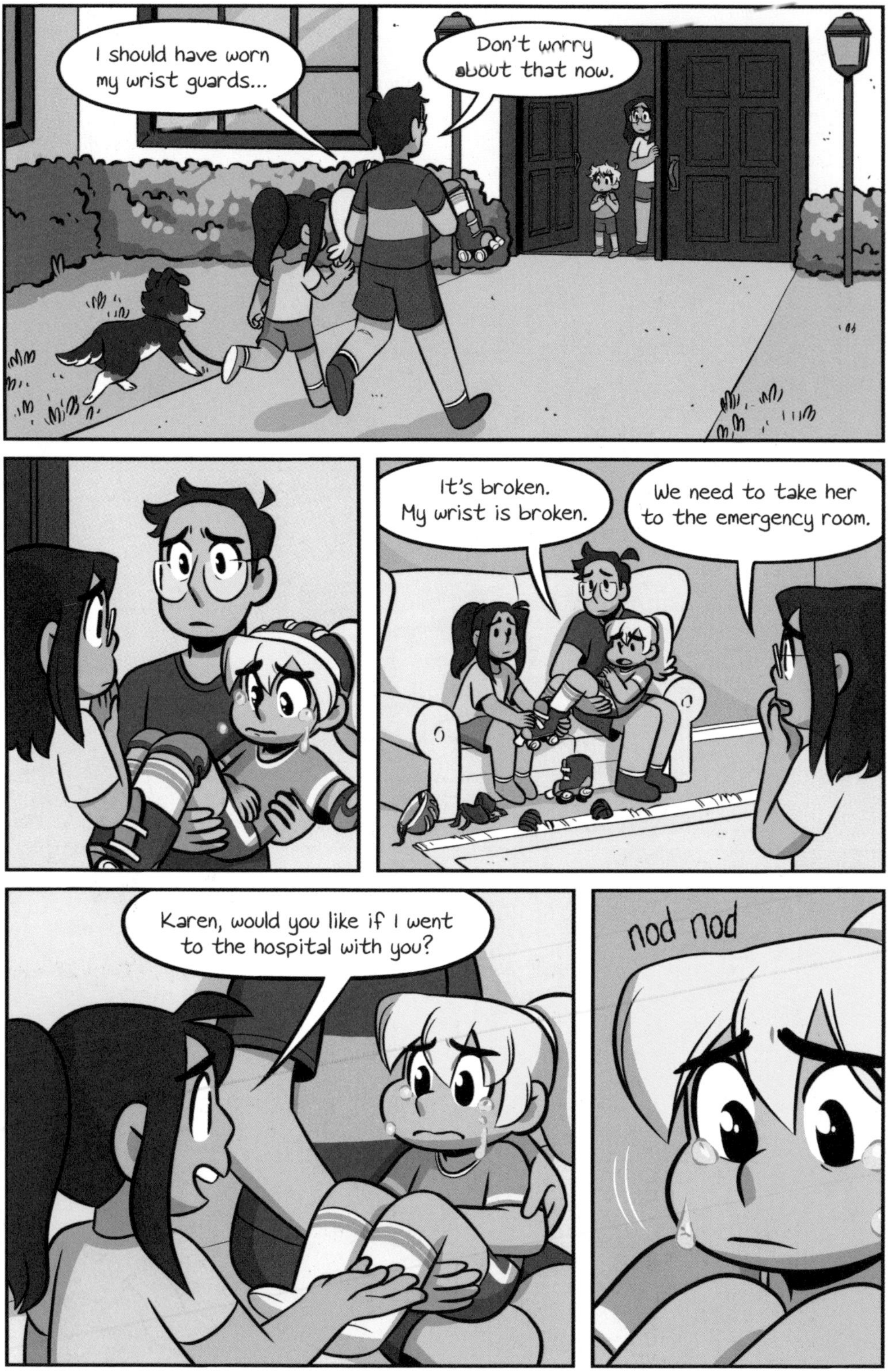
I should have worn my wrist guards...
Don't worry about that now.
It's broken. My wrist is broken.
We need to take her to the emergency room.
Karen, would you like if I went to the hospital with you?
nod nod

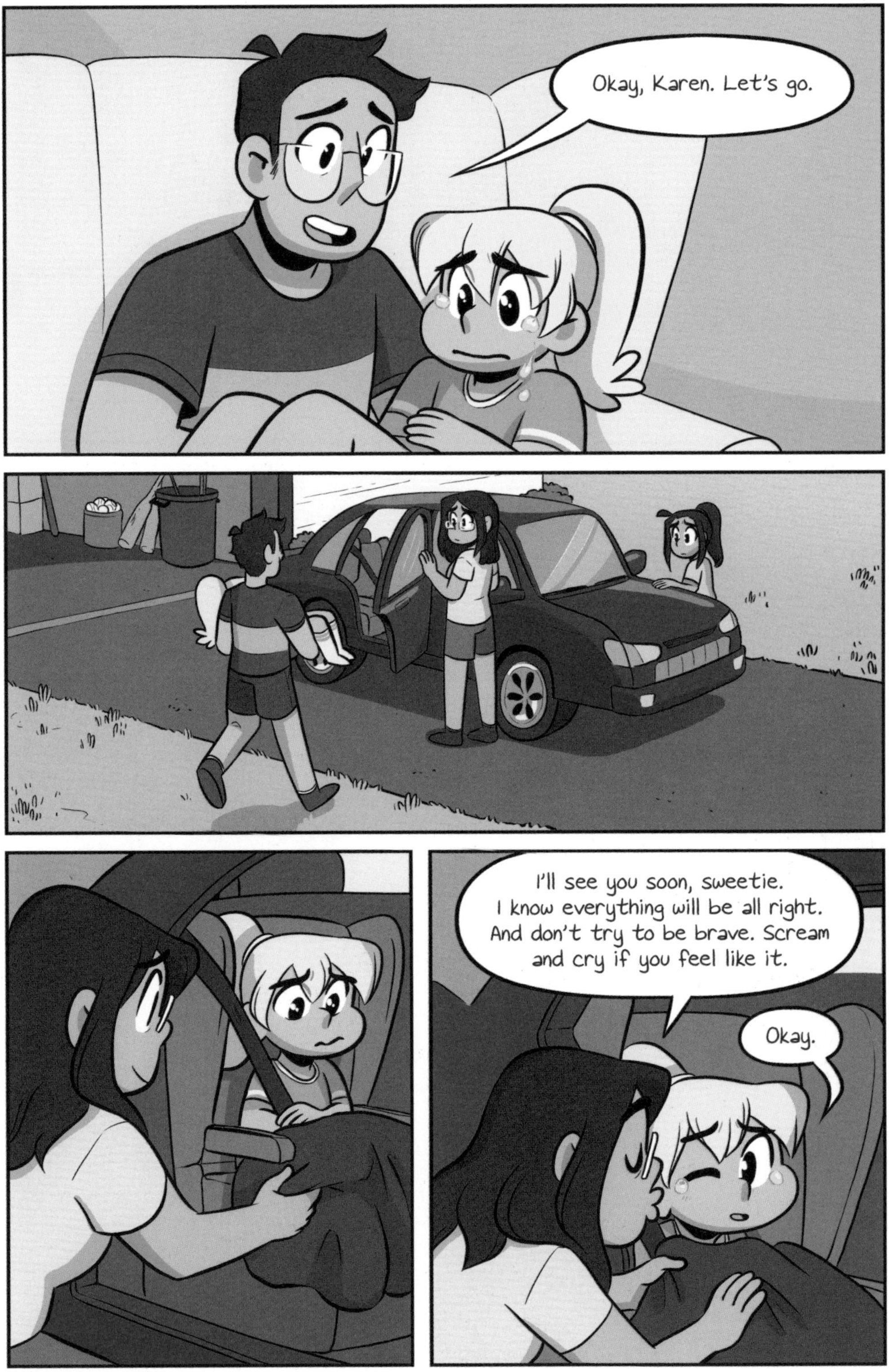
Okay, Karen. Let's go.
I'll see you soon, sweetie. I know everything will be all right. And don't try to be brave. Scream and cry if you feel like it.
Okay.

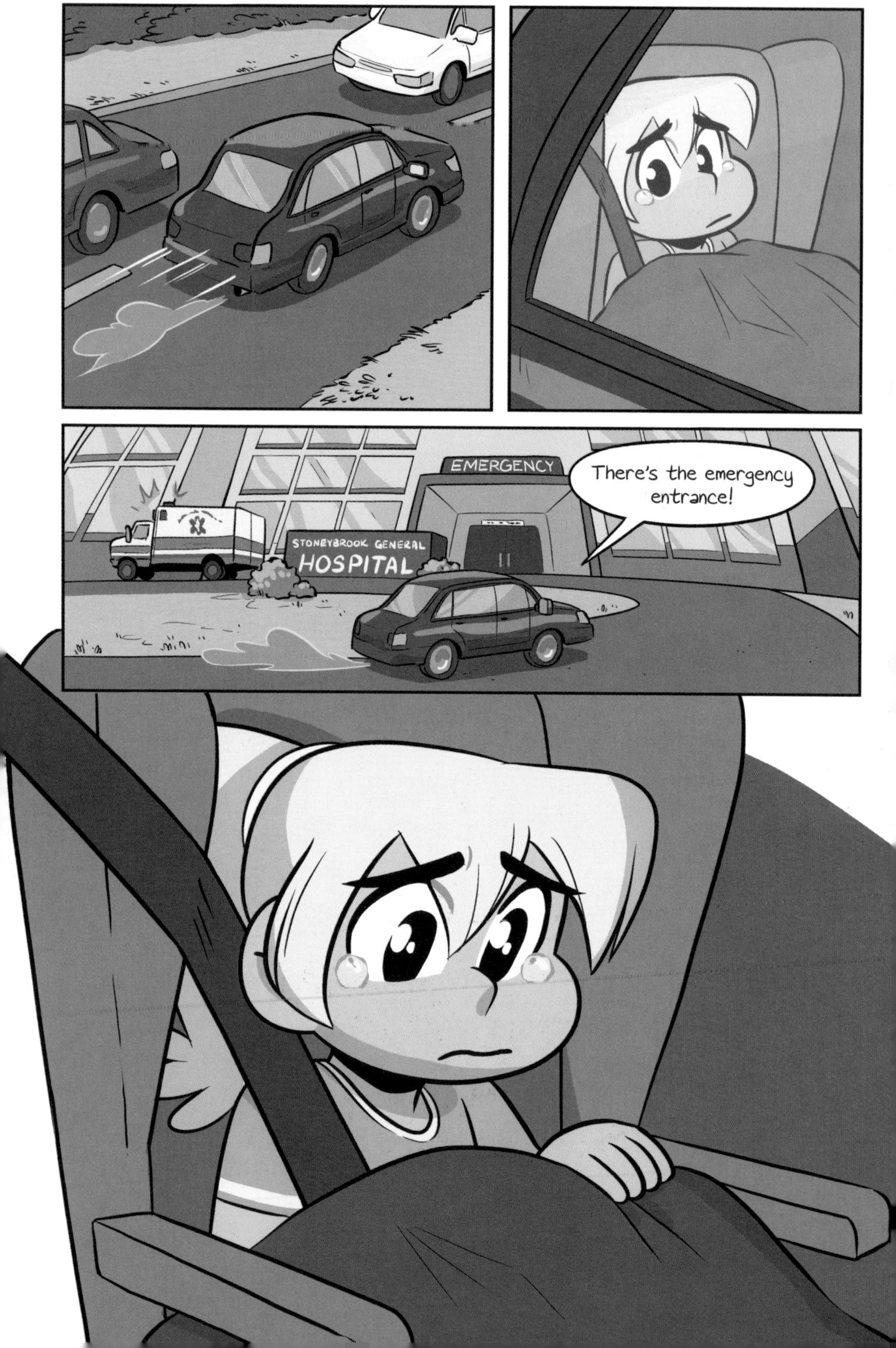
EMERGENCY
STONEYBROOK GENERAL HOSPITAL
There's the emergency entrance!

CHAPTER 3

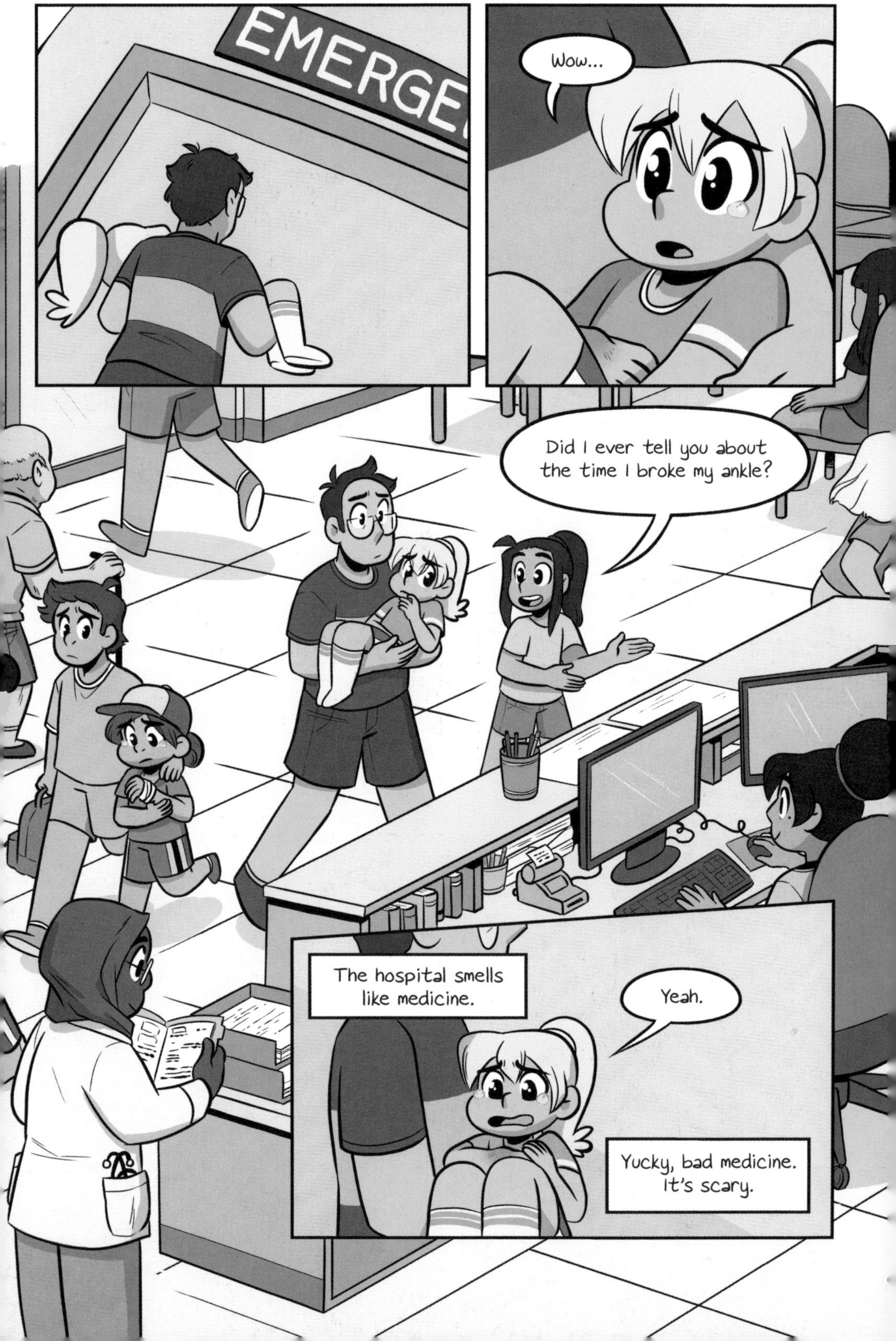
EMERGE
Wow...
Did I ever tell you about the time I broke my ankle?
The hospital smells like medicine.
Yeah.
Yucky, bad medicine. It's scary.

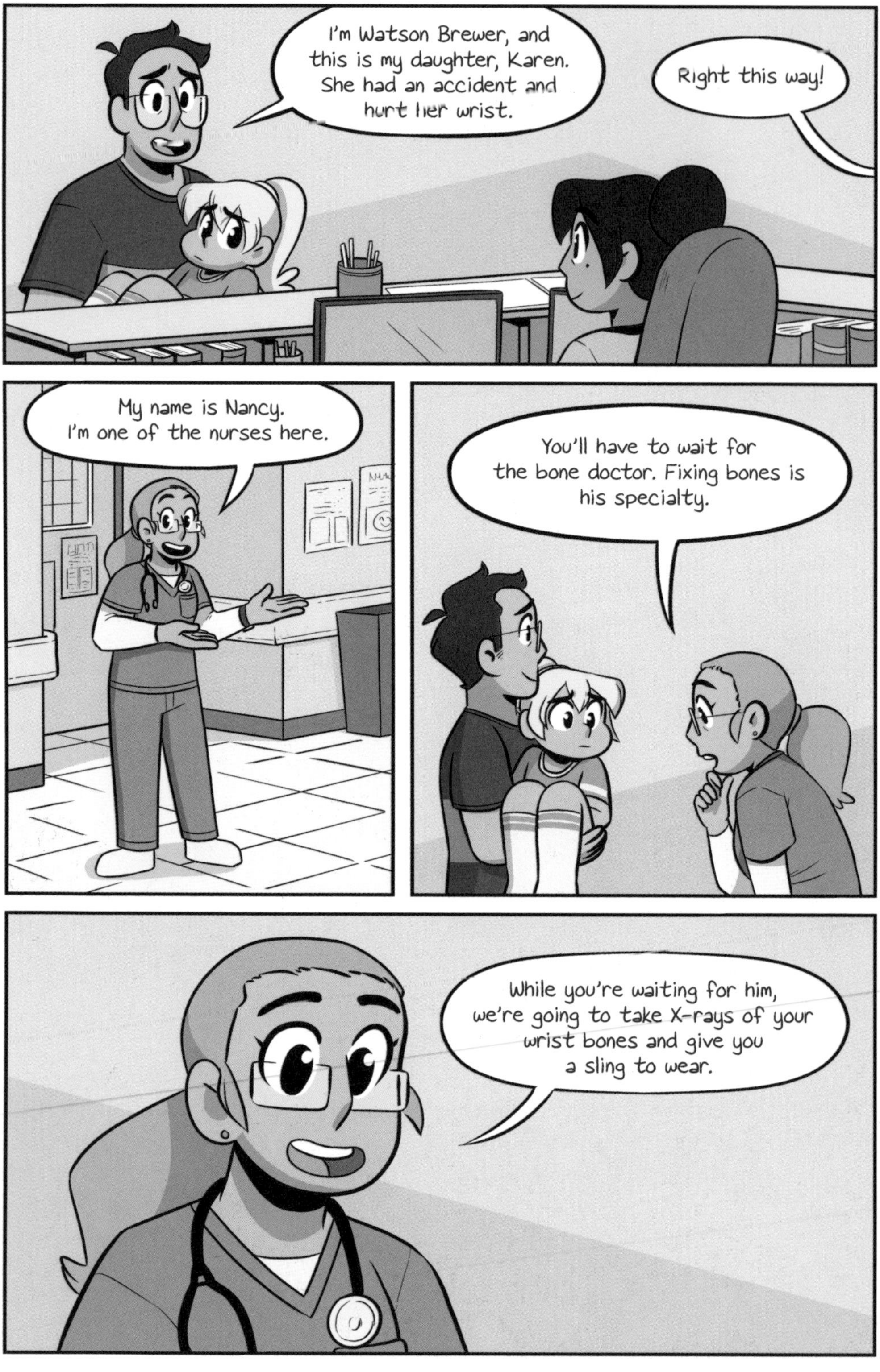
I'm Watson Brewer, and this is my daughter, Karen. She had an accident and hurt her wrist.
Right this way!
My name is Nancy. I'm one of the nurses here.
You'll have to wait for the bone doctor. Fixing bones is his specialty.
While you're waiting for him, we're going to take X-rays of your wrist bones and give you a sling to wear.

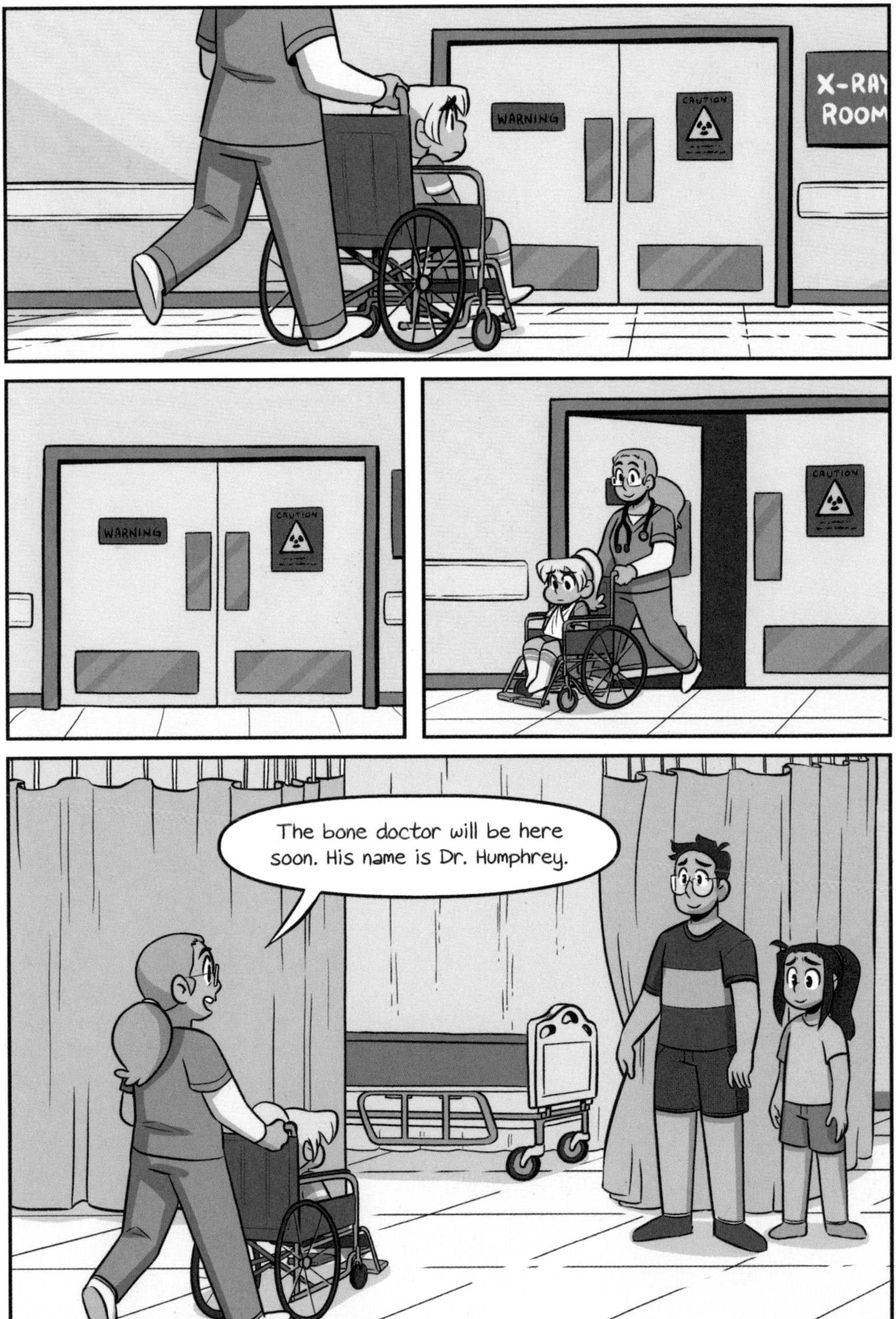
X-RAY ROOM
WARNING
CAUTION
WARNING
CAUTION
CAUTION
The bone doctor will be here soon. His name is Dr. Humphrey.

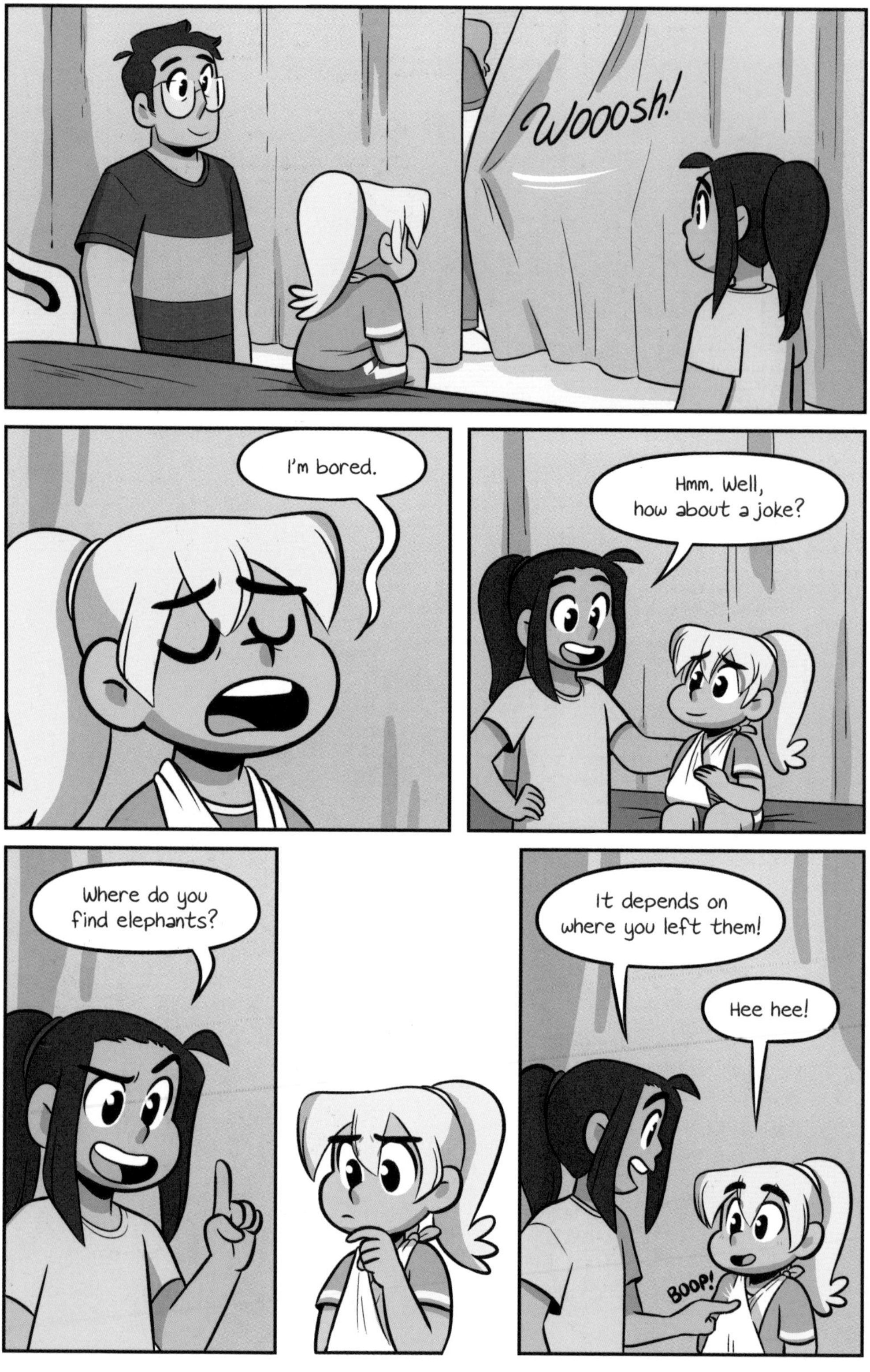
Wooosh!
I'm bored.
Hmm. Well, how about a joke?
Where do you find elephants?
It depends on where you left them!
Hee hee!
BOOP!

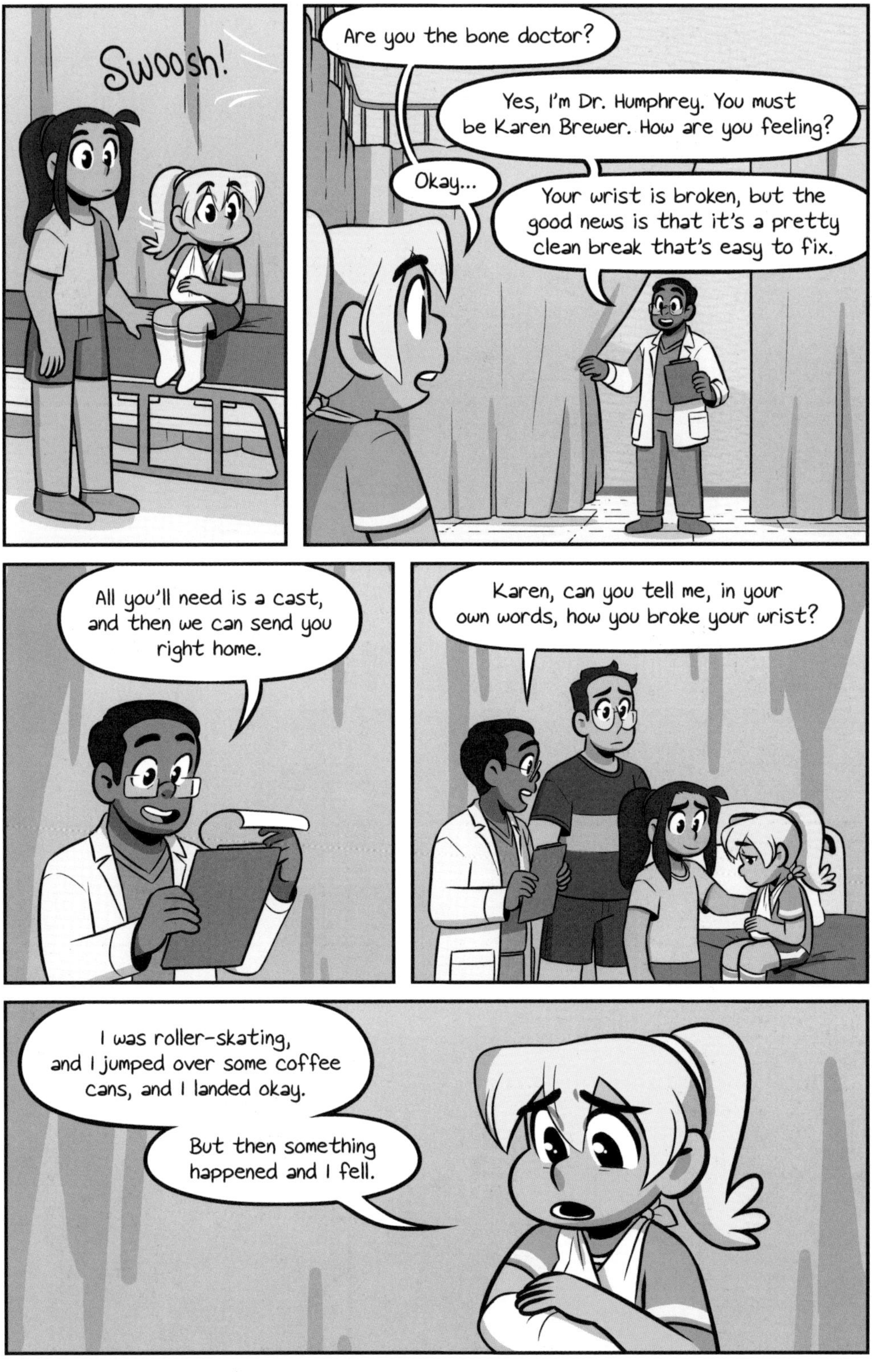
Swoosh!
Are you the bone doctor?
Yes, I'm Dr. Humphrey. You must be Karen Brewer. How are you feeling?
Okay...
Your wrist is broken, but the good news is that it's a pretty clean break that's easy to fix.
All you'll need is a cast, and then we can send you right home.
Karen, can you tell me, in your own words, how you broke your wrist?
I was roller-skating, and I jumped over some coffee cans, and I landed okay.
But then something happened and I fell.

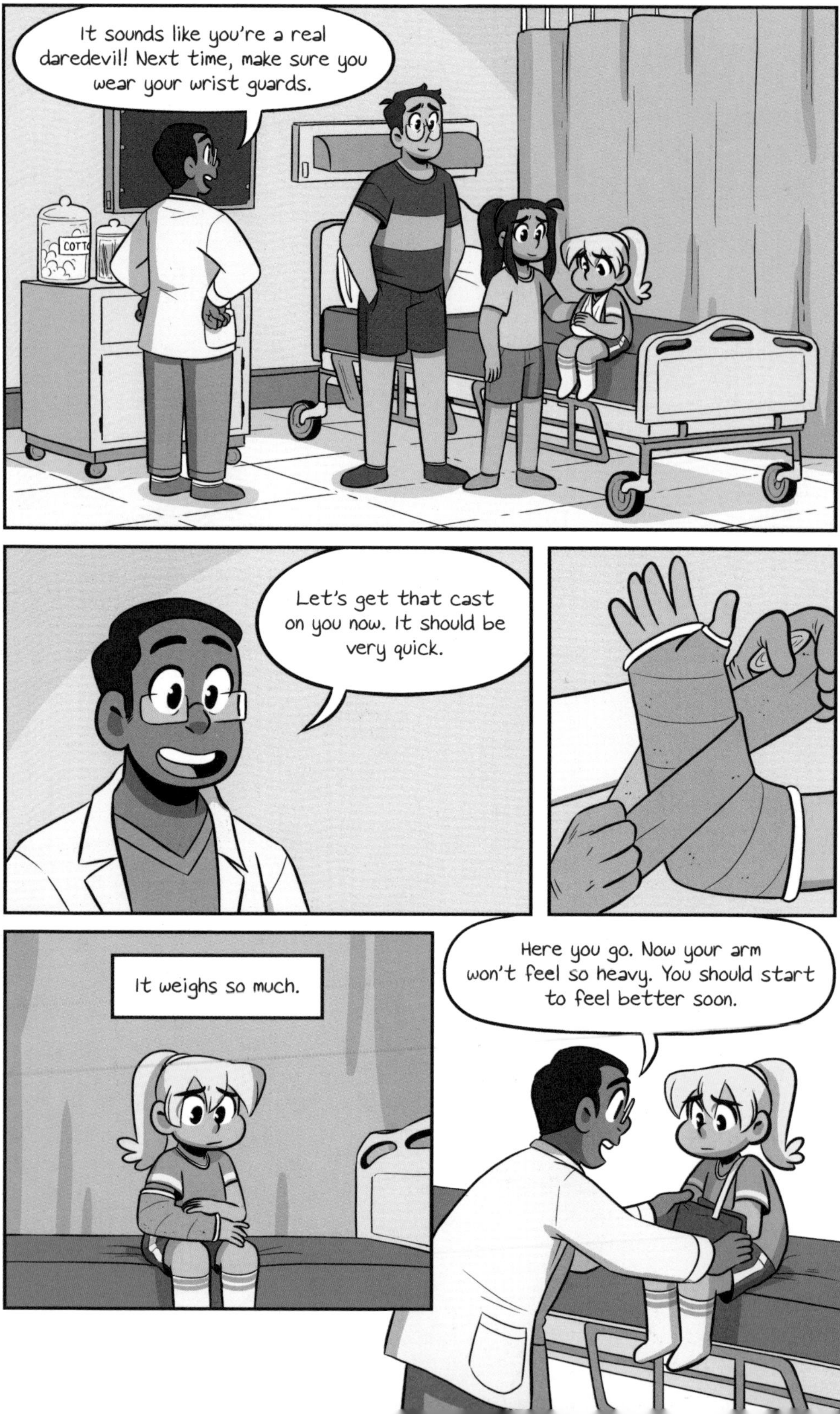
It sounds like you're a real daredevil! Next time, make sure you wear your wrist guards.
COTTO
Let's get that cast on you now. It should be very quick.
It weighs so much.
Here you go. Now your arm won't feel so heavy. You should start to feel better soon.

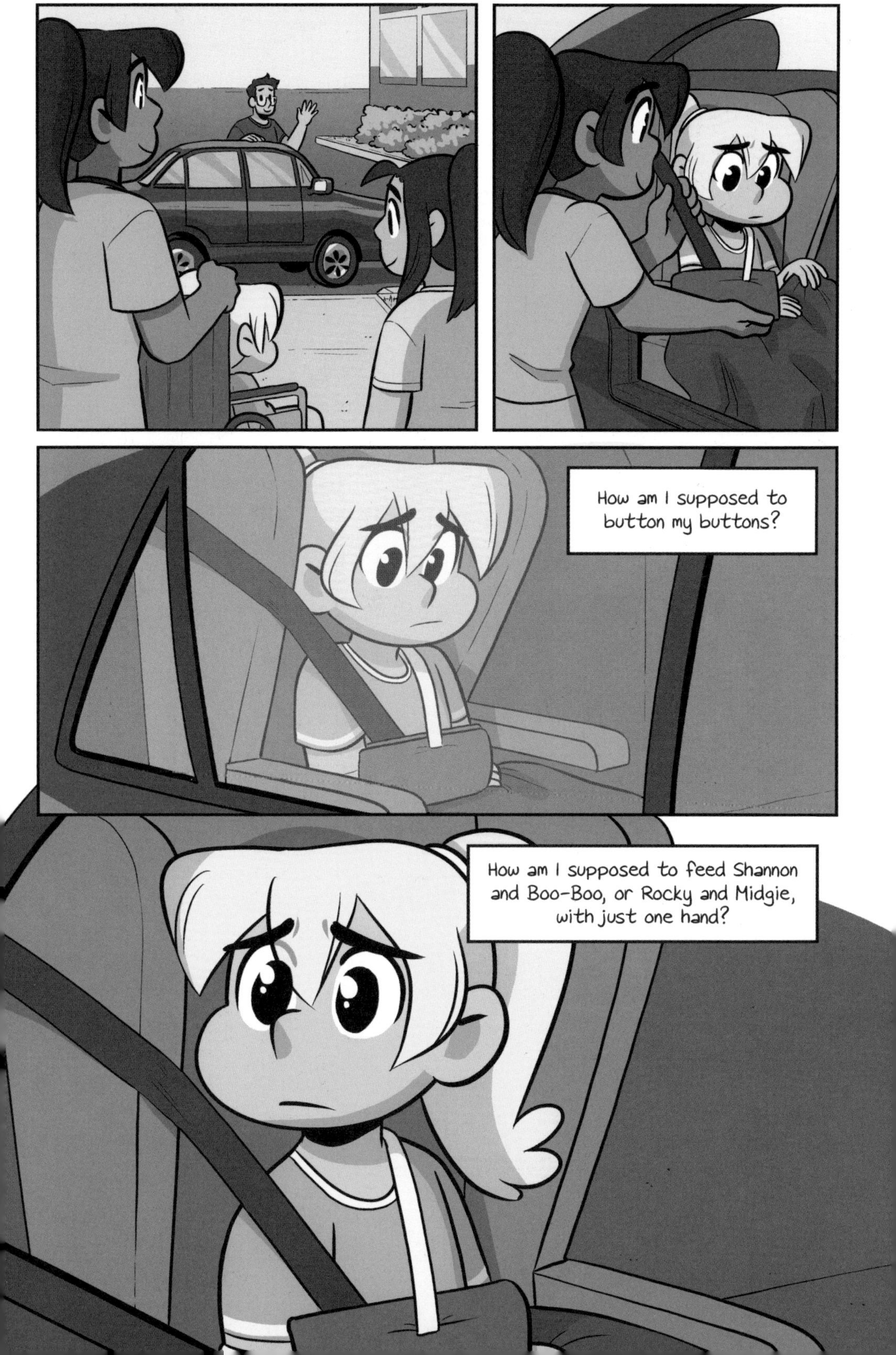
How am I supposed to button my buttons?
How am I supposed to feed Shannon and Boo-Boo, or Rocky and Midgie, with just one hand?

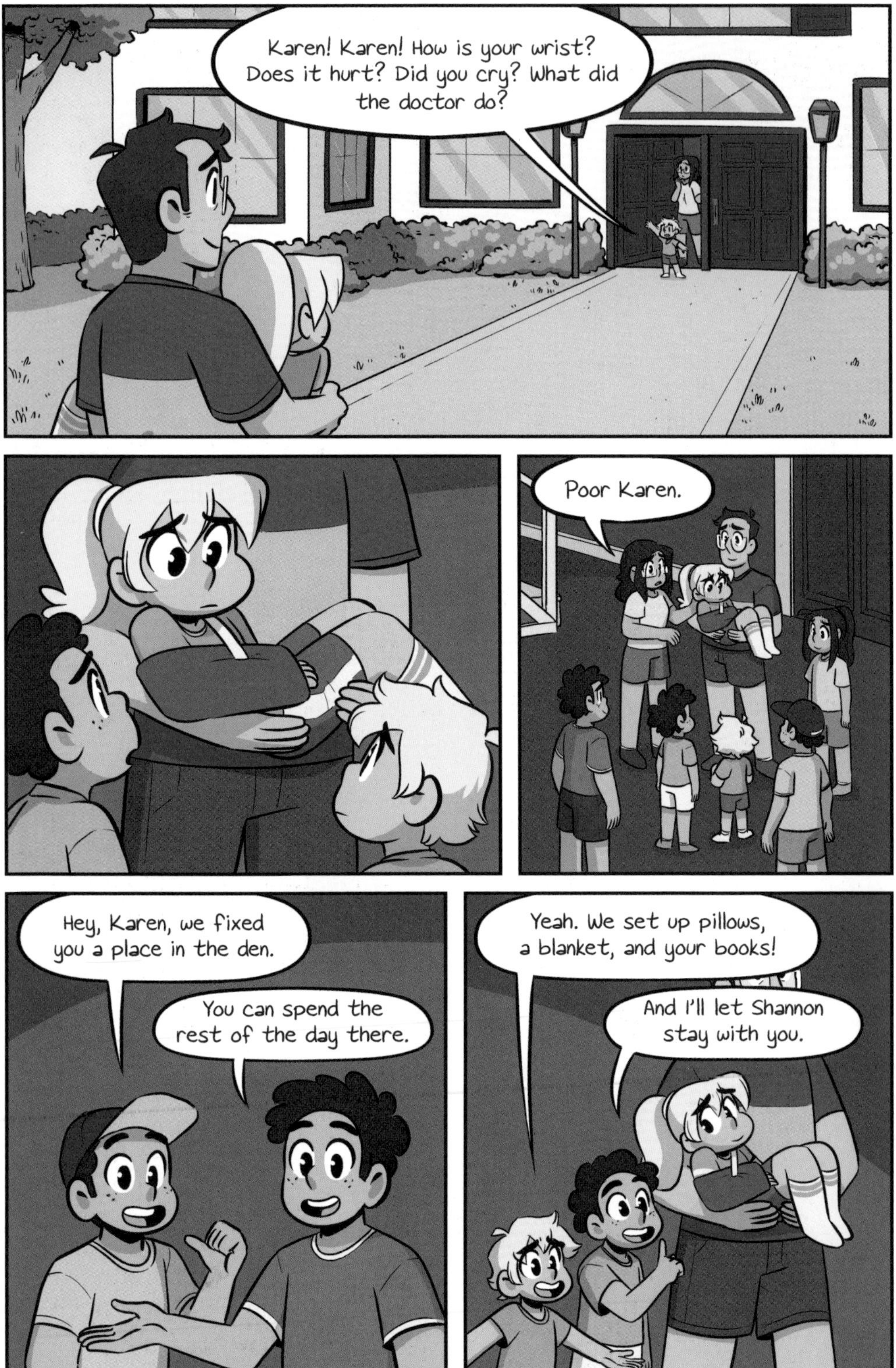
Karen! Karen! How is your wrist? Does it hurt? Did you cry? What did the doctor do?
Poor Karen.
Hey, Karen, we fixed you a place in the den.
You can spend the rest of the day there.
Yeah. We set up pillows, a blanket, and your books!
And I'll let Shannon stay with you.

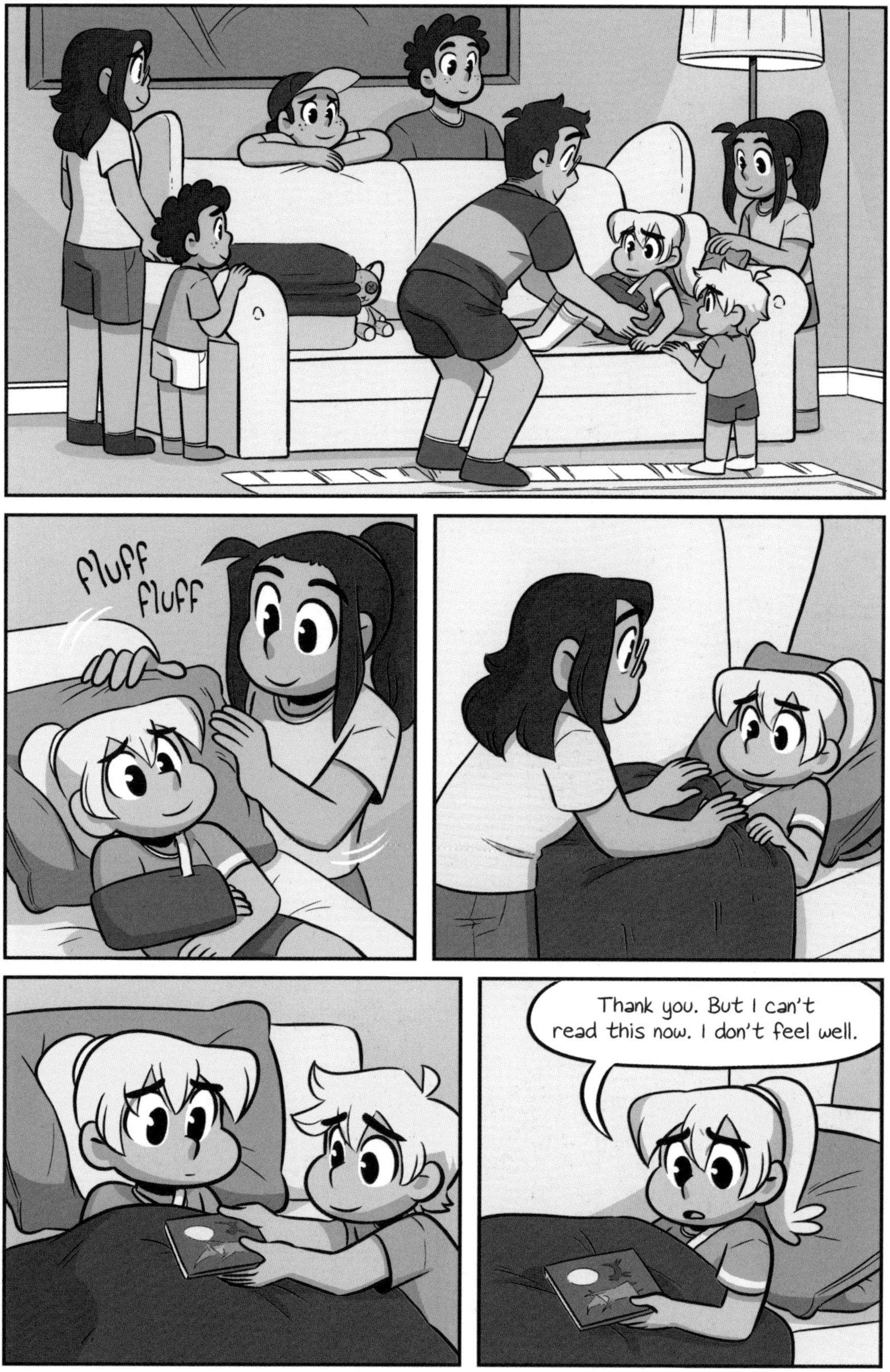
fluff
fluff
Thank you. But I can't read this now. I don't feel well.

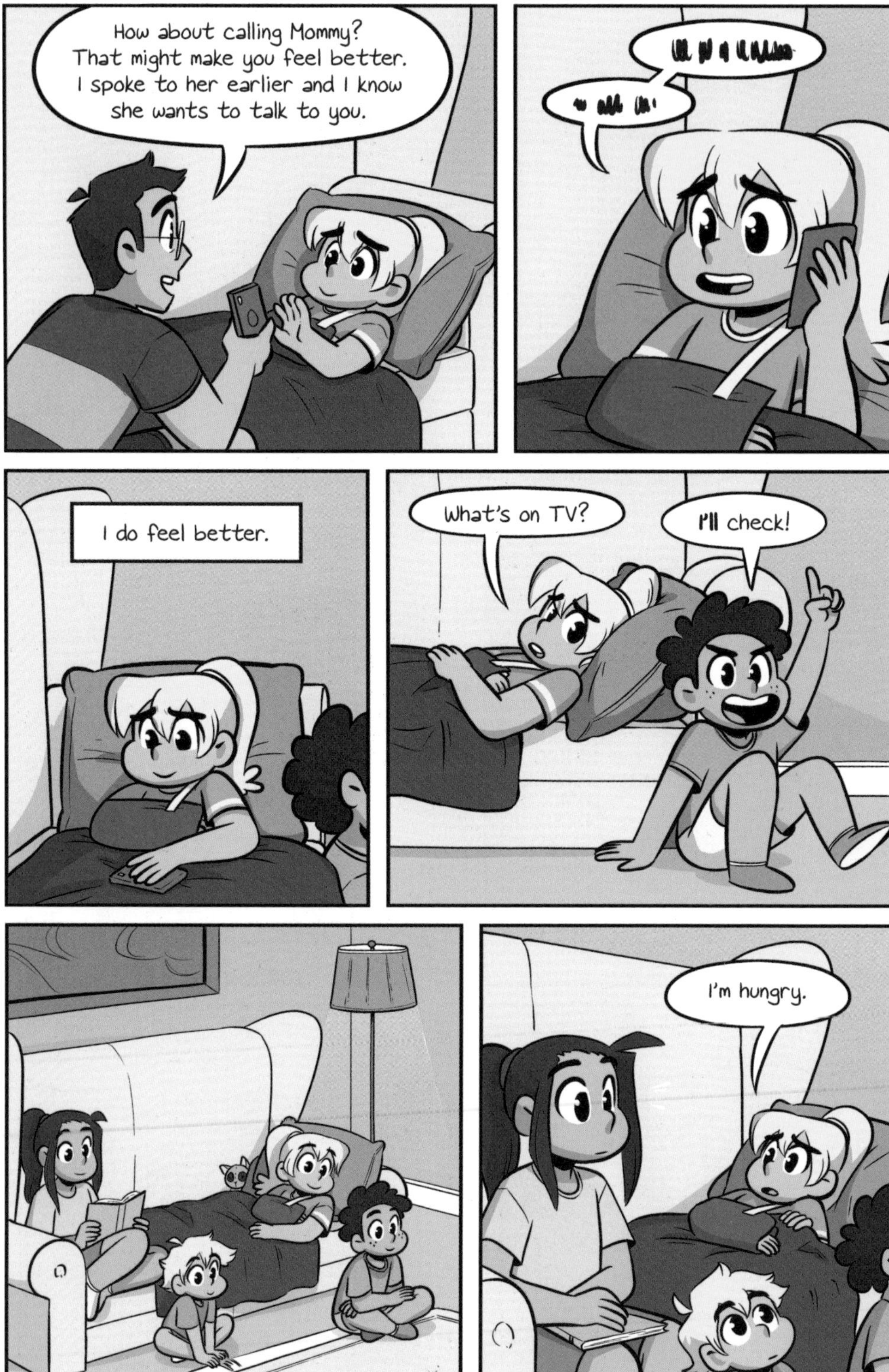
How about calling Mommy? That might make you feel better. I spoke to her earlier and I know she wants to talk to you.
I do feel better.
What's on TV?
I'll check!
I'm hungry.

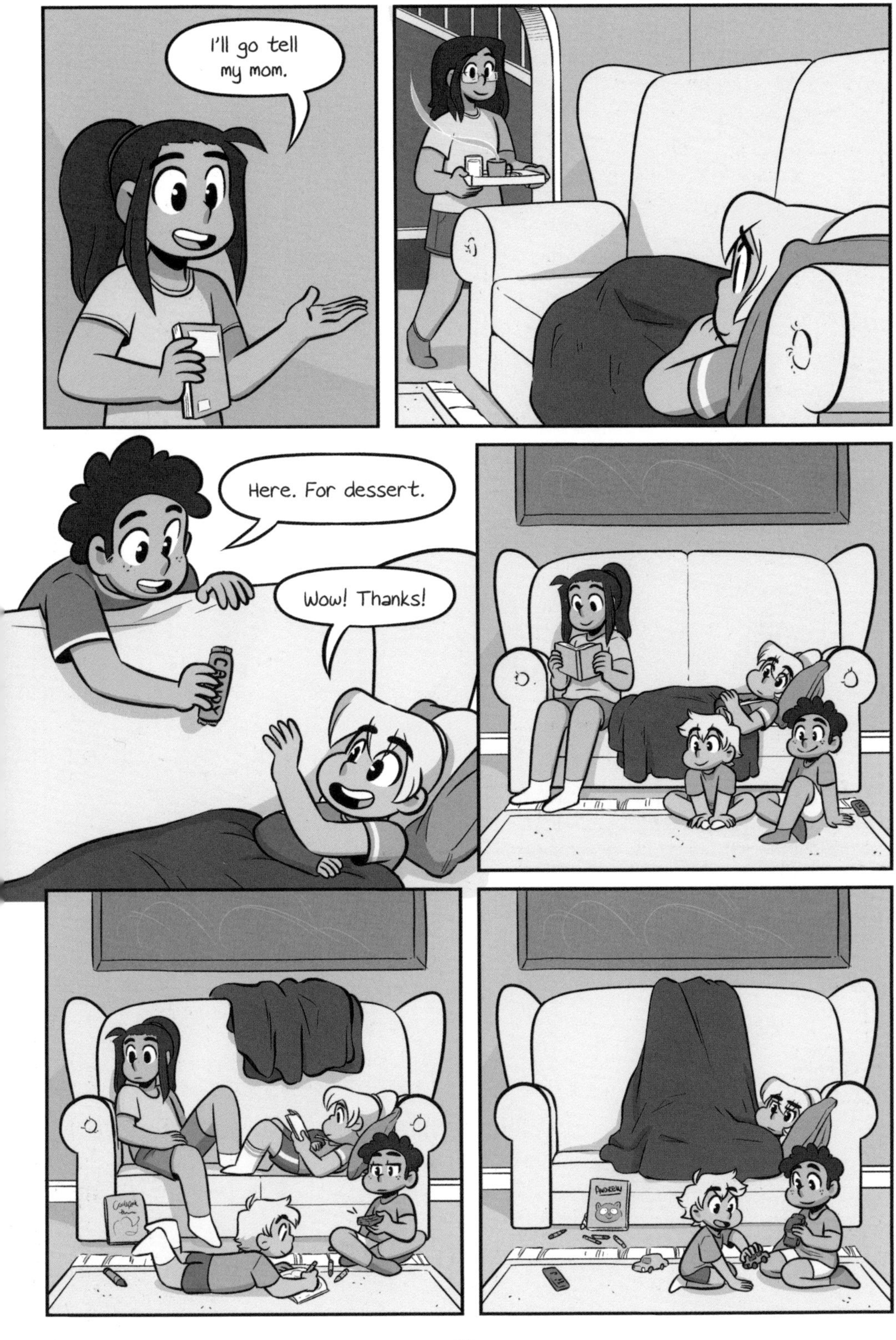
I'll go tell my mom.
Here. For dessert.
CANDY
Wow! Thanks!
ANDREW

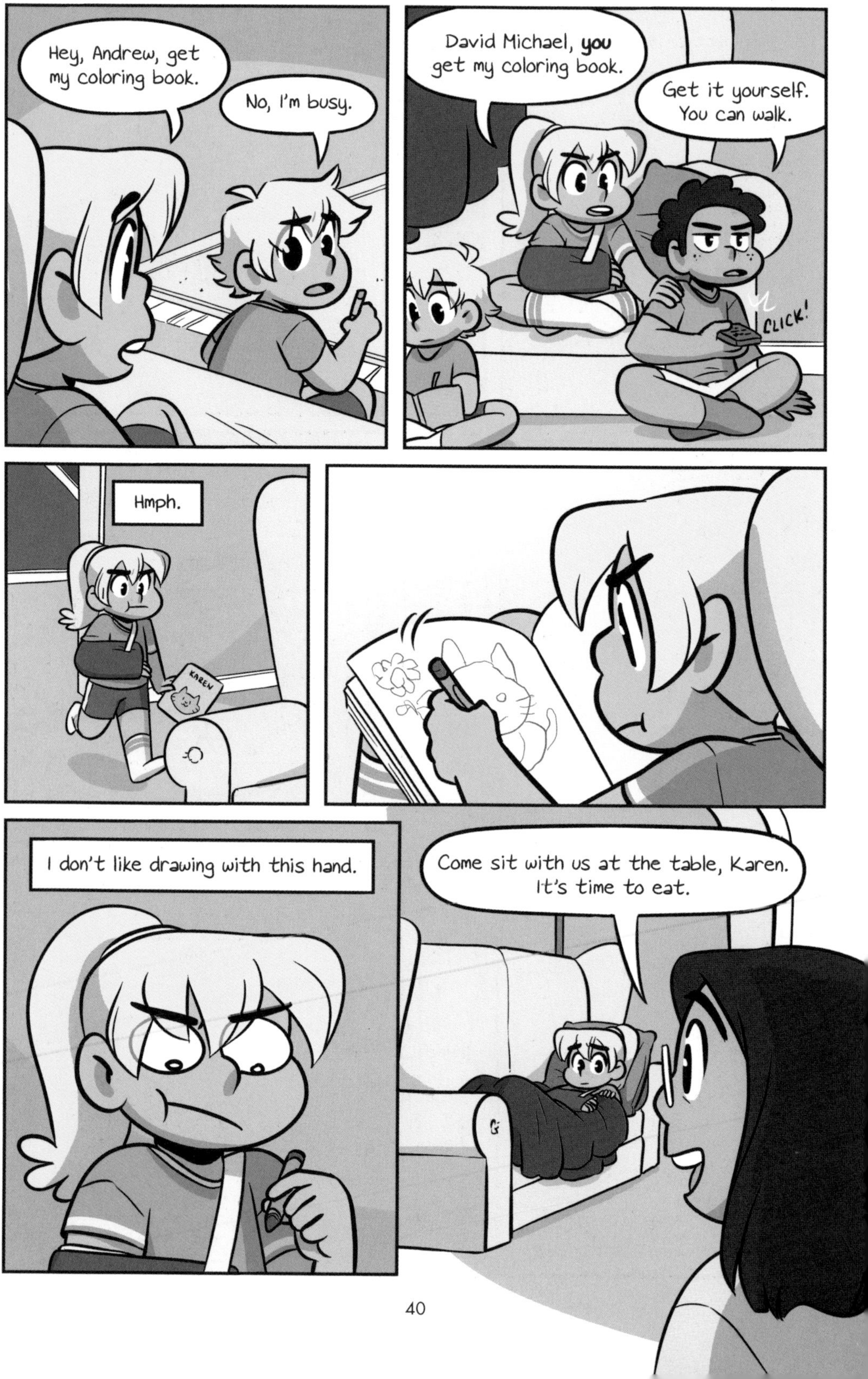
Hey, Andrew, get my coloring book.
No, I'm busy.
David Michael, **you** get my coloring book.
Get it yourself. You can walk.
CLICK!
Hmph.
KAREN
I don't like drawing with this hand.
Come sit with us at the table, Karen. It's time to eat.

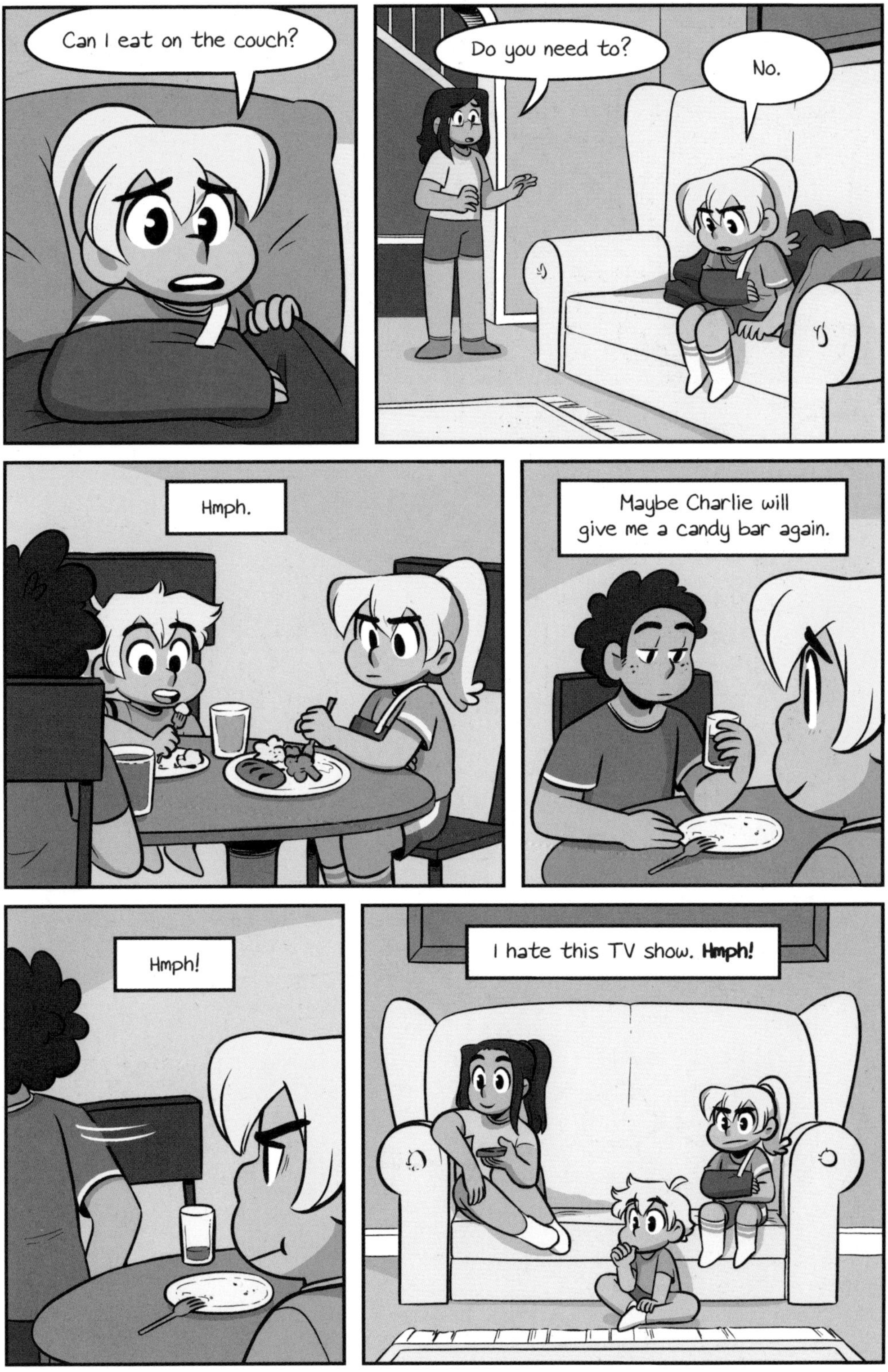
Can I eat on the couch?
Do you need to?
No.
Hmph.
Maybe Charlie will give me a candy bar again.
Hmph!
I hate this TV show. **Hmph!**

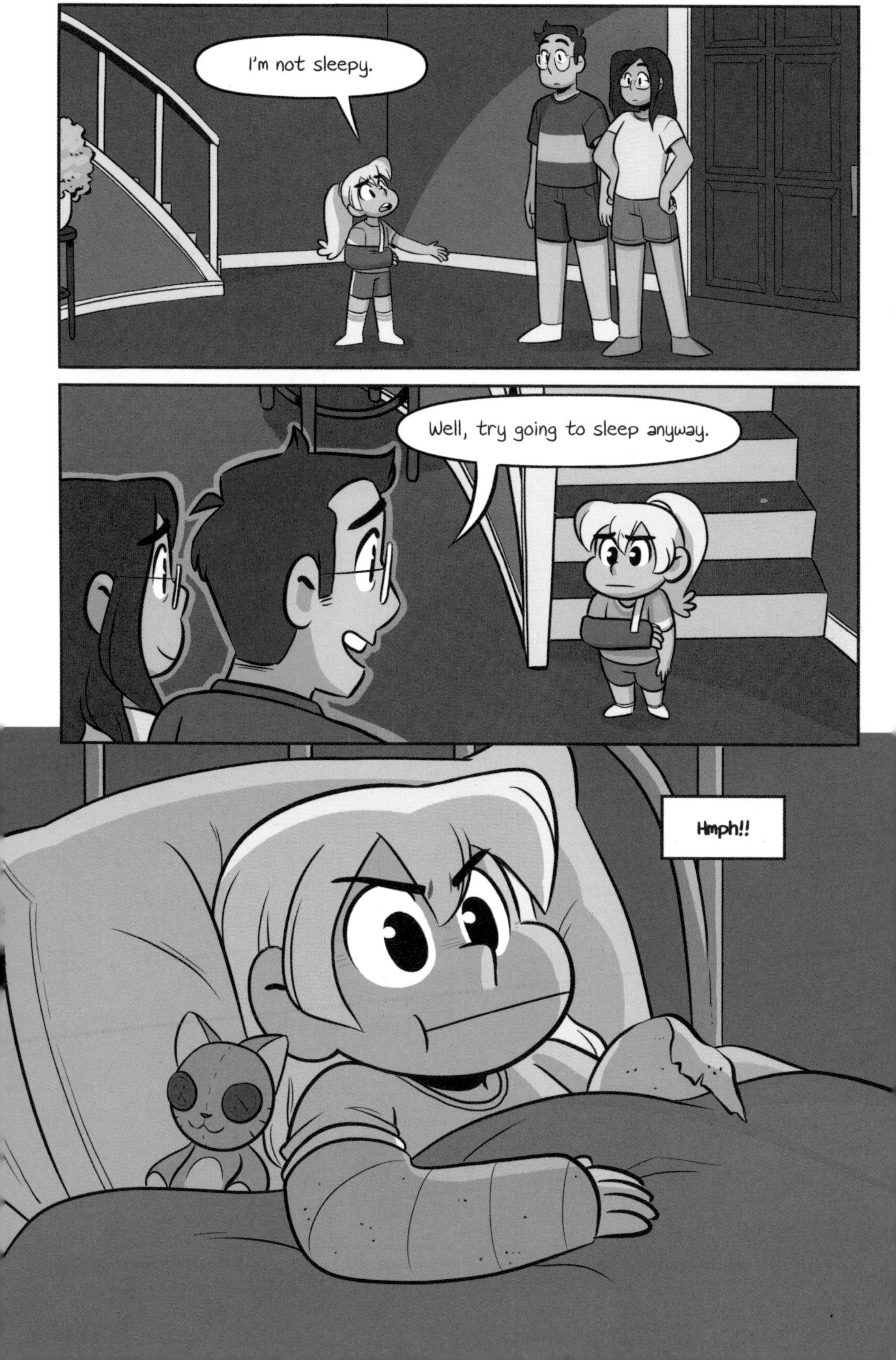
I'm not sleepy.
Well, try going to sleep anyway.
Hmph!!

CHAPTER 4

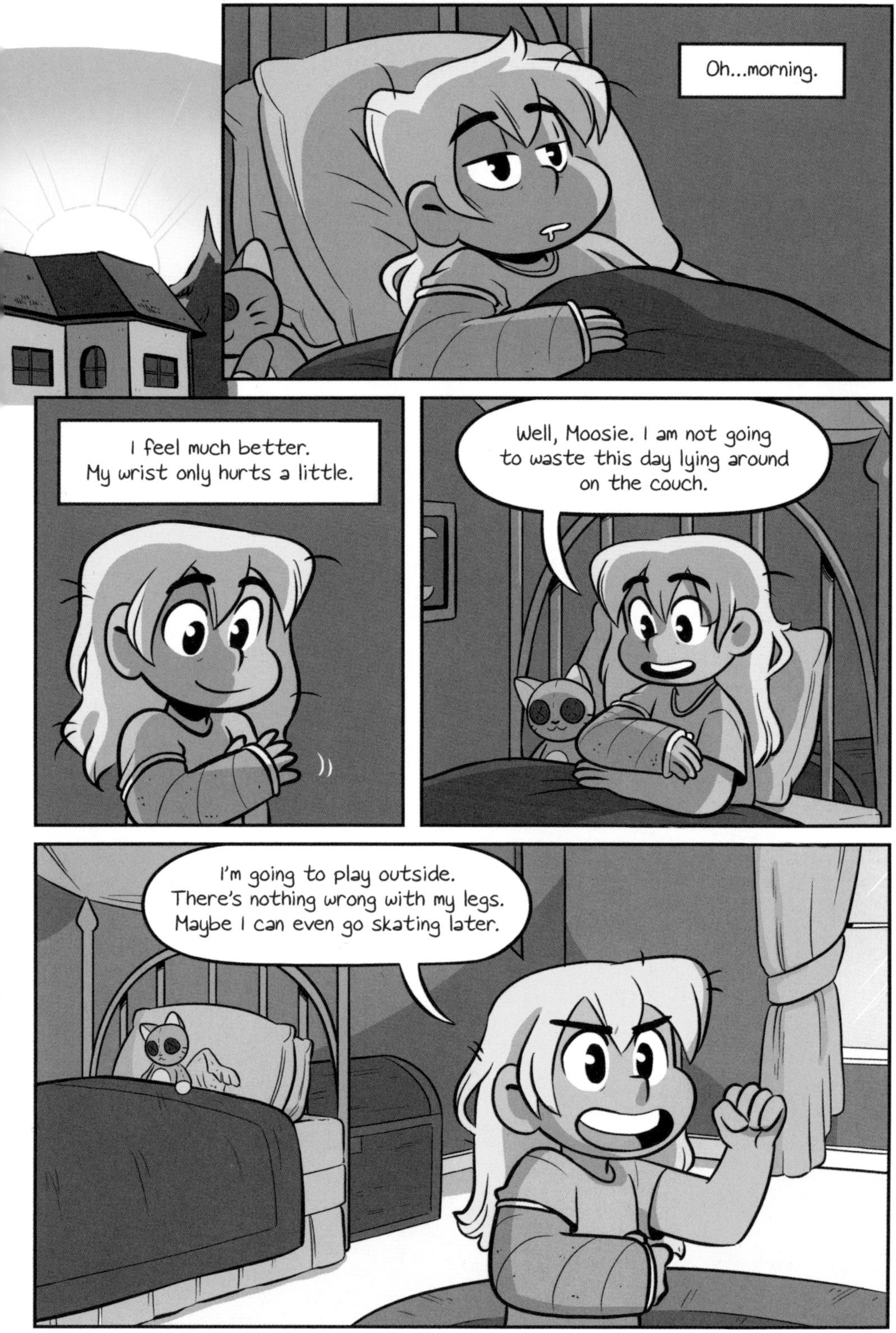

Oh...morning.
I feel much better.
My wrist only hurts a little.
Well, Moosie. I am not going to waste this day lying around on the couch.
I'm going to play outside. There's nothing wrong with my legs. Maybe I can even go skating later.

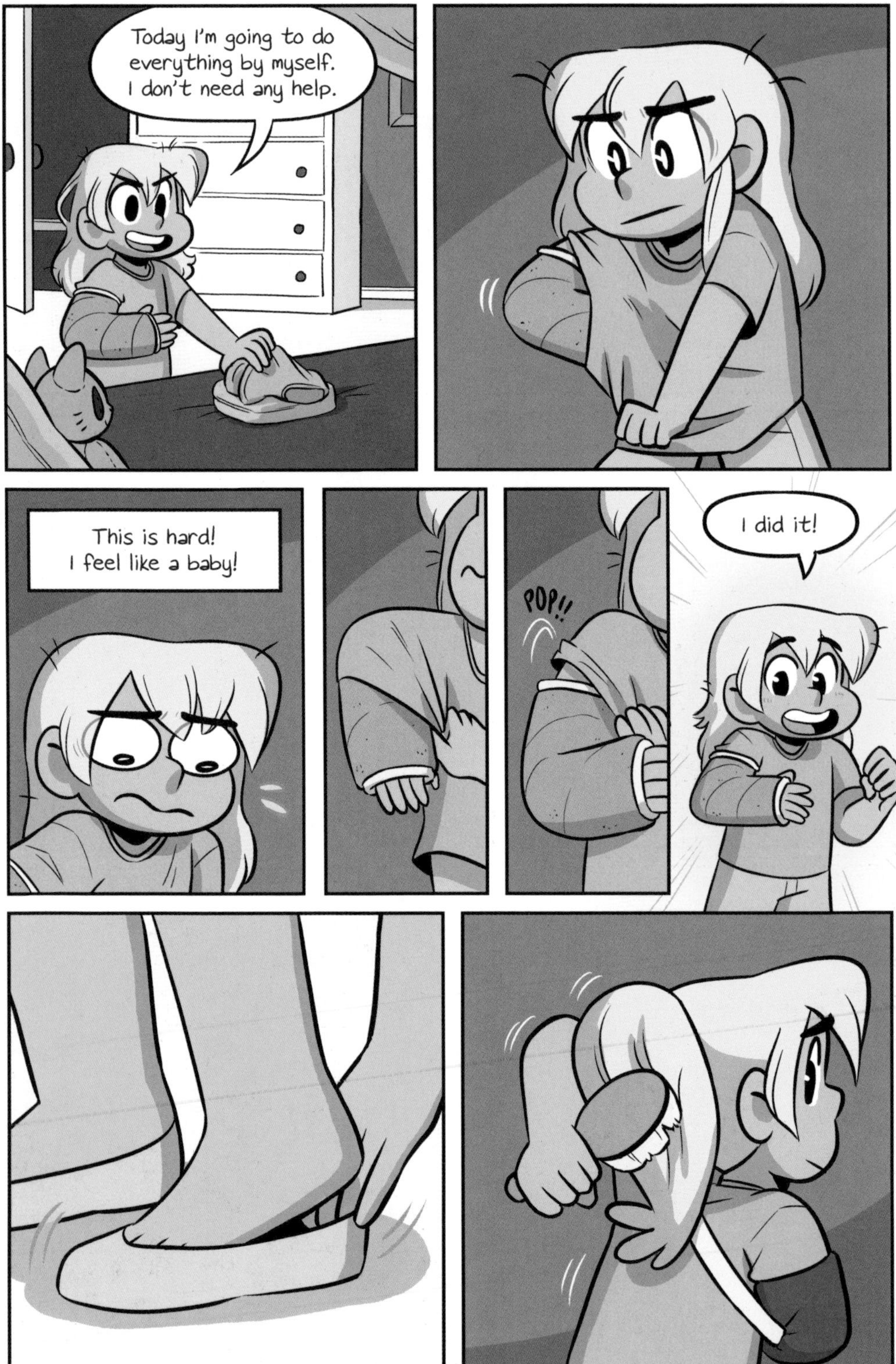
Today I'm going to do everything by myself. I don't need any help.
This is hard! I feel like a baby!
POP!!
I did it!

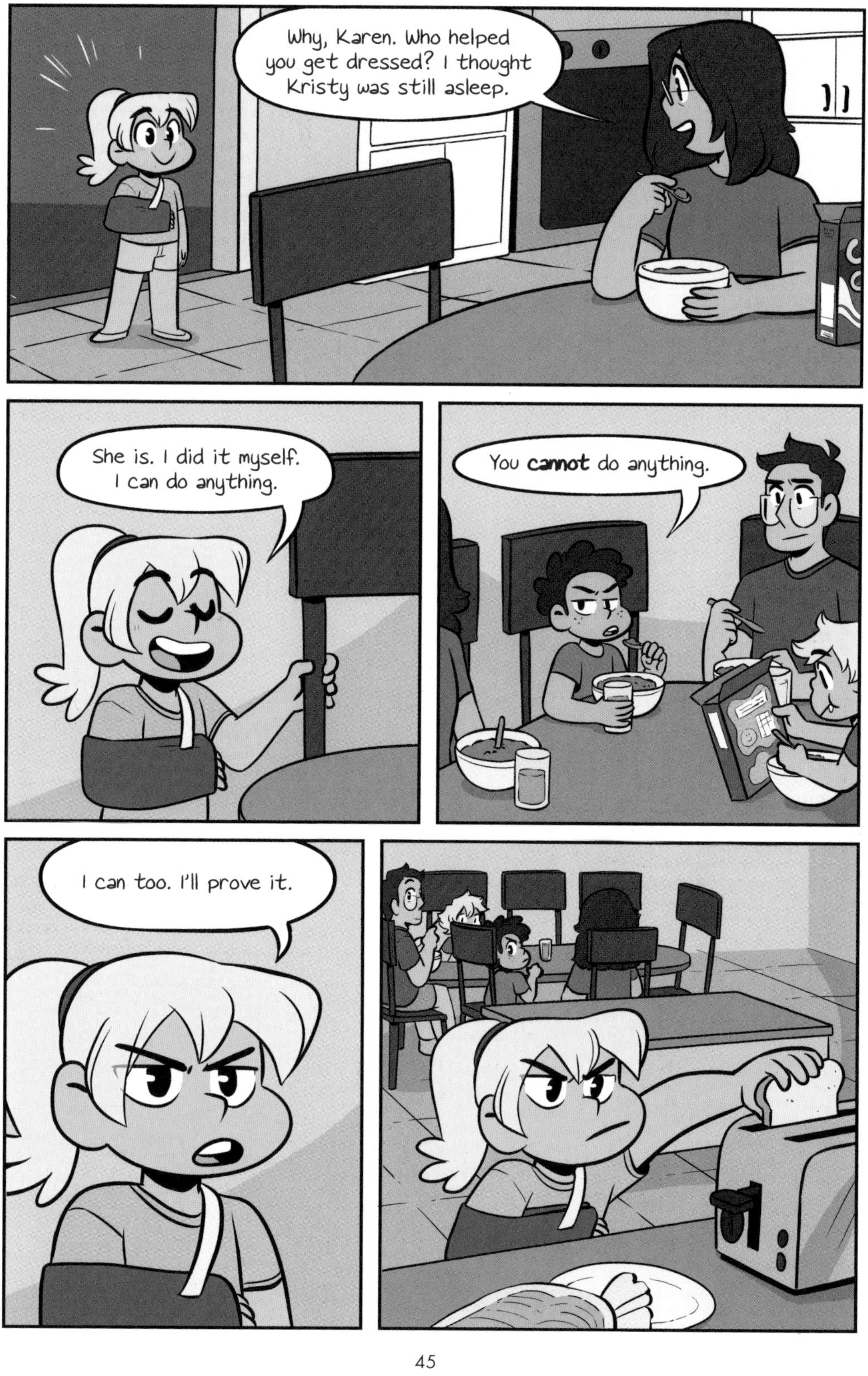
Why, Karen. Who helped you get dressed? I thought Kristy was still asleep.
She is. I did it myself. I can do anything.
You **cannot** do anything.
I can too. I'll prove it.

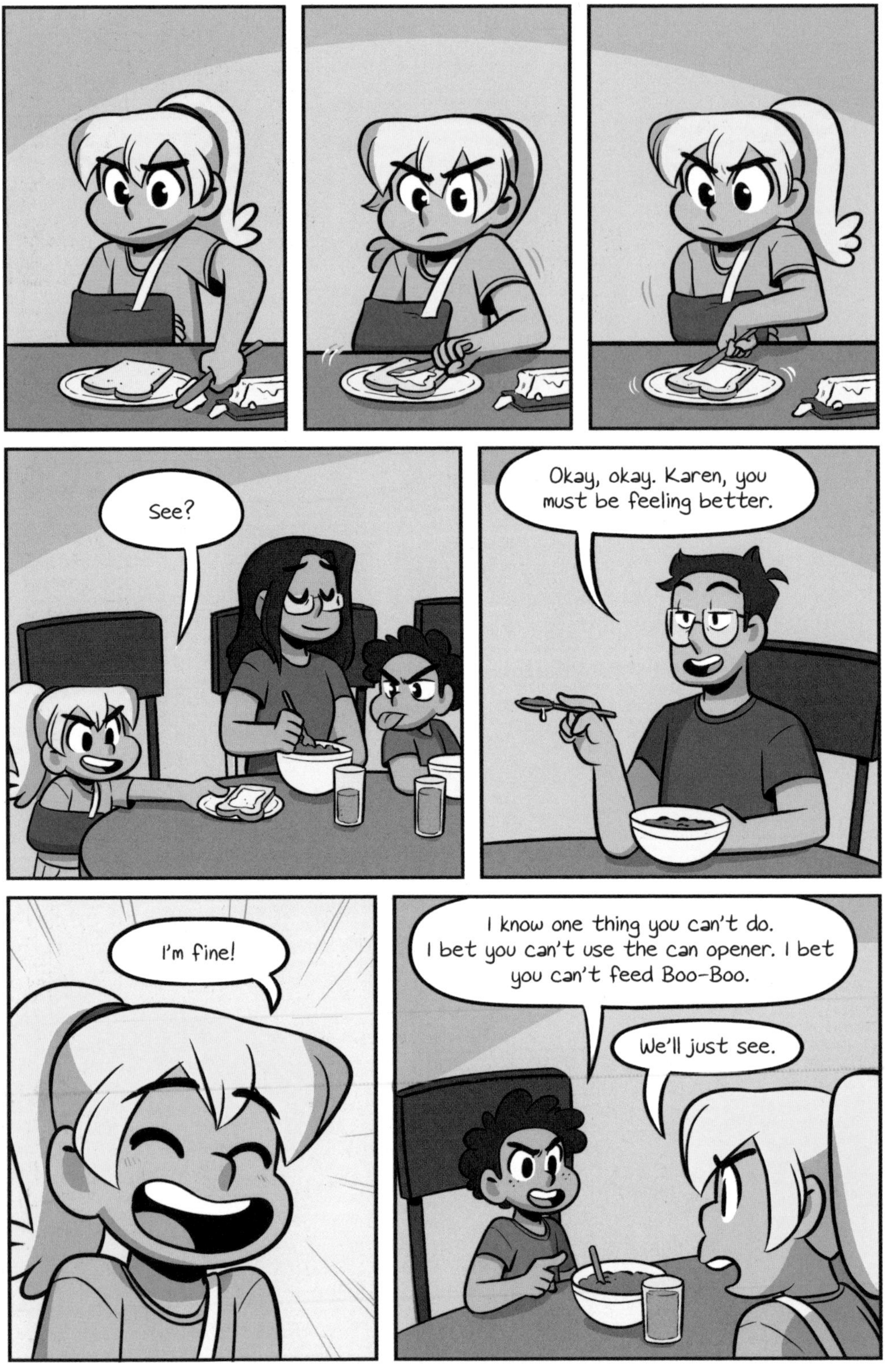
See?
Okay, okay. Karen, you must be feeling better.
I'm fine!
I know one thing you can't do. I bet you can't use the can opener. I bet you can't feed Boo-Boo.
We'll just see.

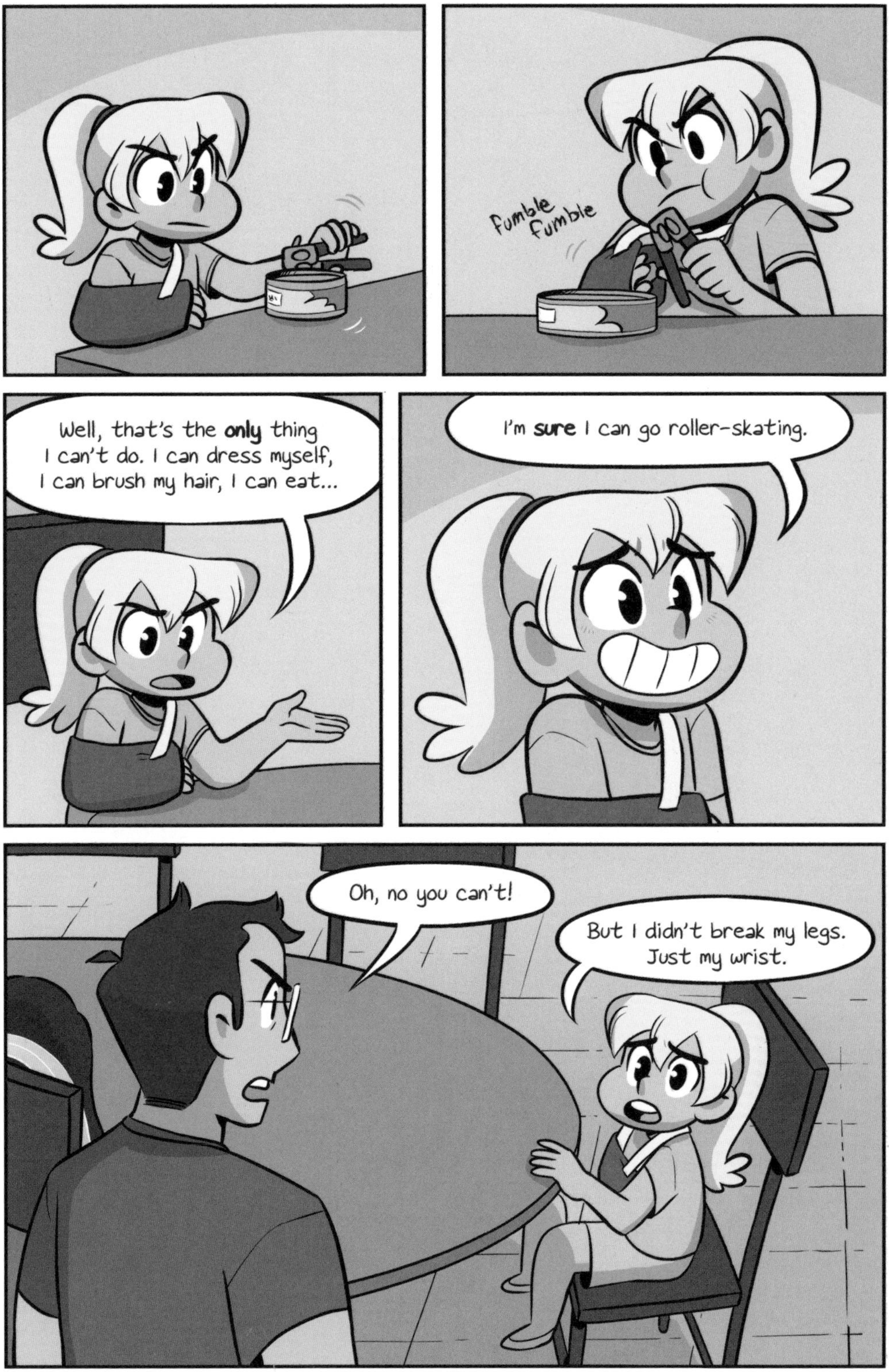
fumble fumble
Well, that's the **only** thing I can't do. I can dress myself, I can brush my hair, I can eat...
I'm **sure** I can go roller-skating.
Oh, no you can't!
But I didn't break my legs. Just my wrist.

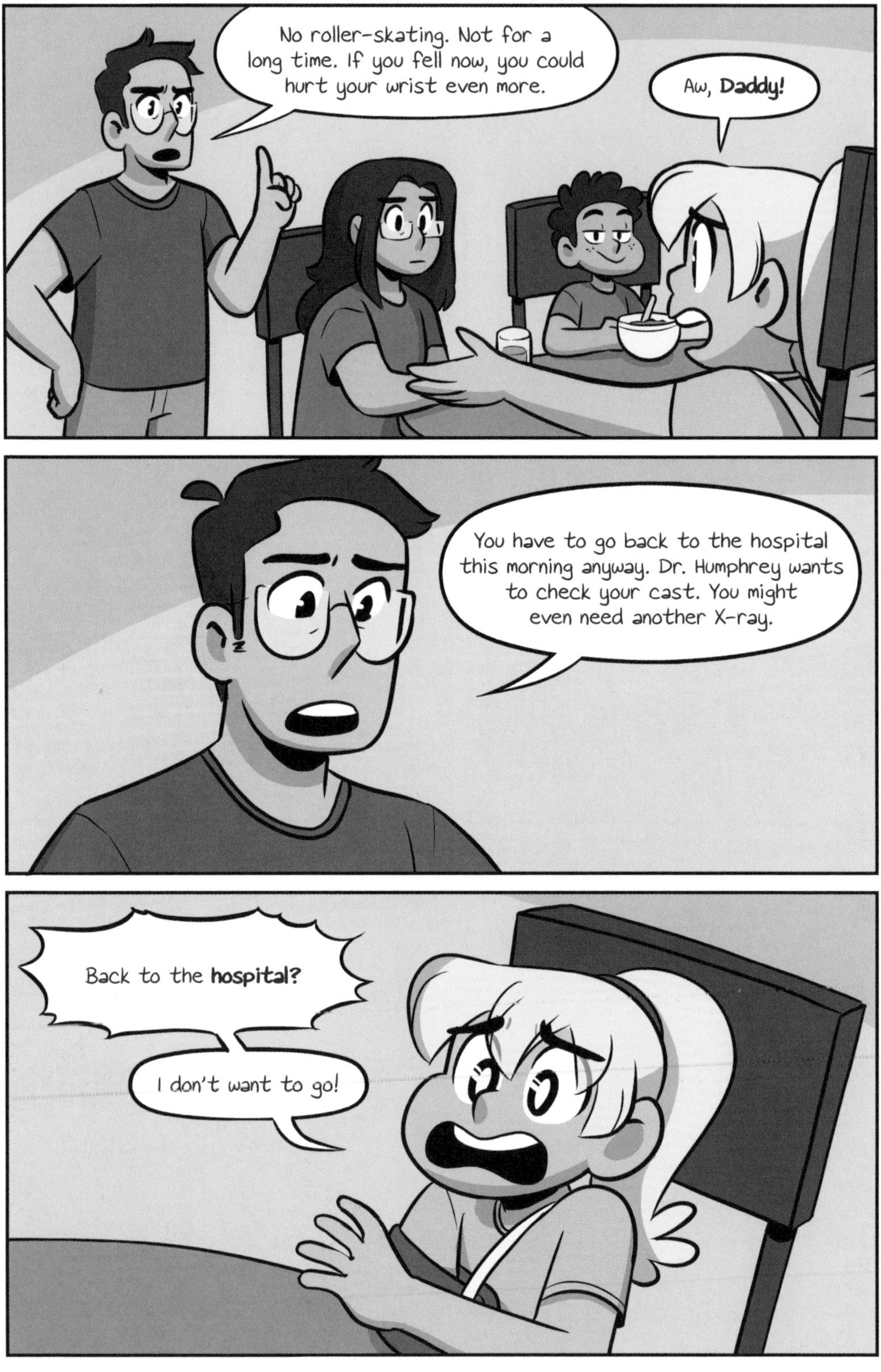
No roller-skating. Not for a long time. If you fell now, you could hurt your wrist even more.
Aw, **Daddy!**
You have to go back to the hospital this morning anyway. Dr. Humphrey wants to check your cast. You might even need another X-ray.
Back to the **hospital?**
I don't want to go!

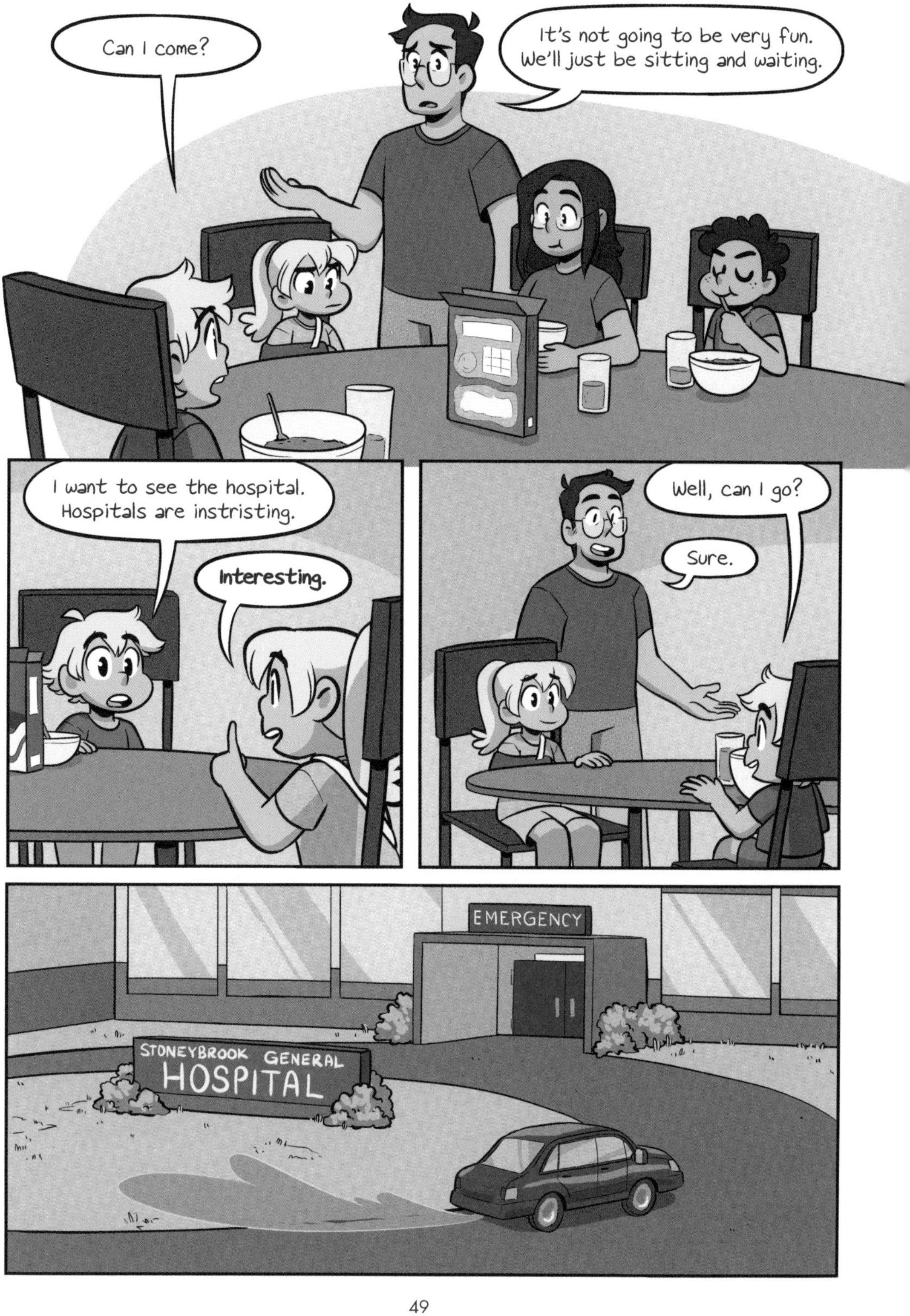
Can I come?
It's not going to be very fun. We'll just be sitting and waiting.
I want to see the hospital. Hospitals are instristing.
Interesting.
Well, can I go?
Sure.
EMERGENCY
STONEYBROOK GENERAL HOSPITAL

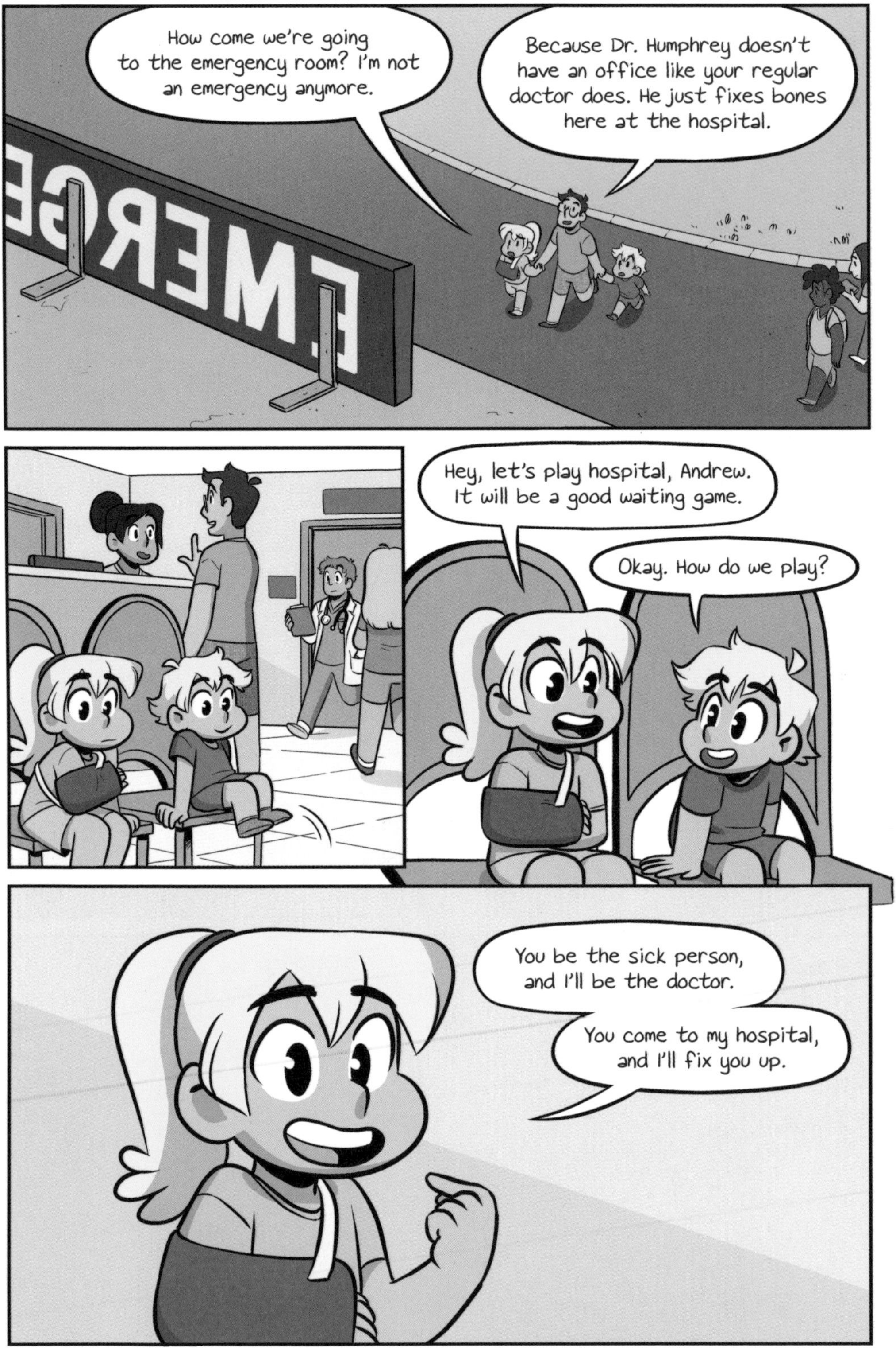
How come we're going to the emergency room? I'm not an emergency anymore.
Because Dr. Humphrey doesn't have an office like your regular doctor does. He just fixes bones here at the hospital.
Hey, let's play hospital, Andrew. It will be a good waiting game.
Okay. How do we play?
You be the sick person, and I'll be the doctor.
You come to my hospital, and I'll fix you up.

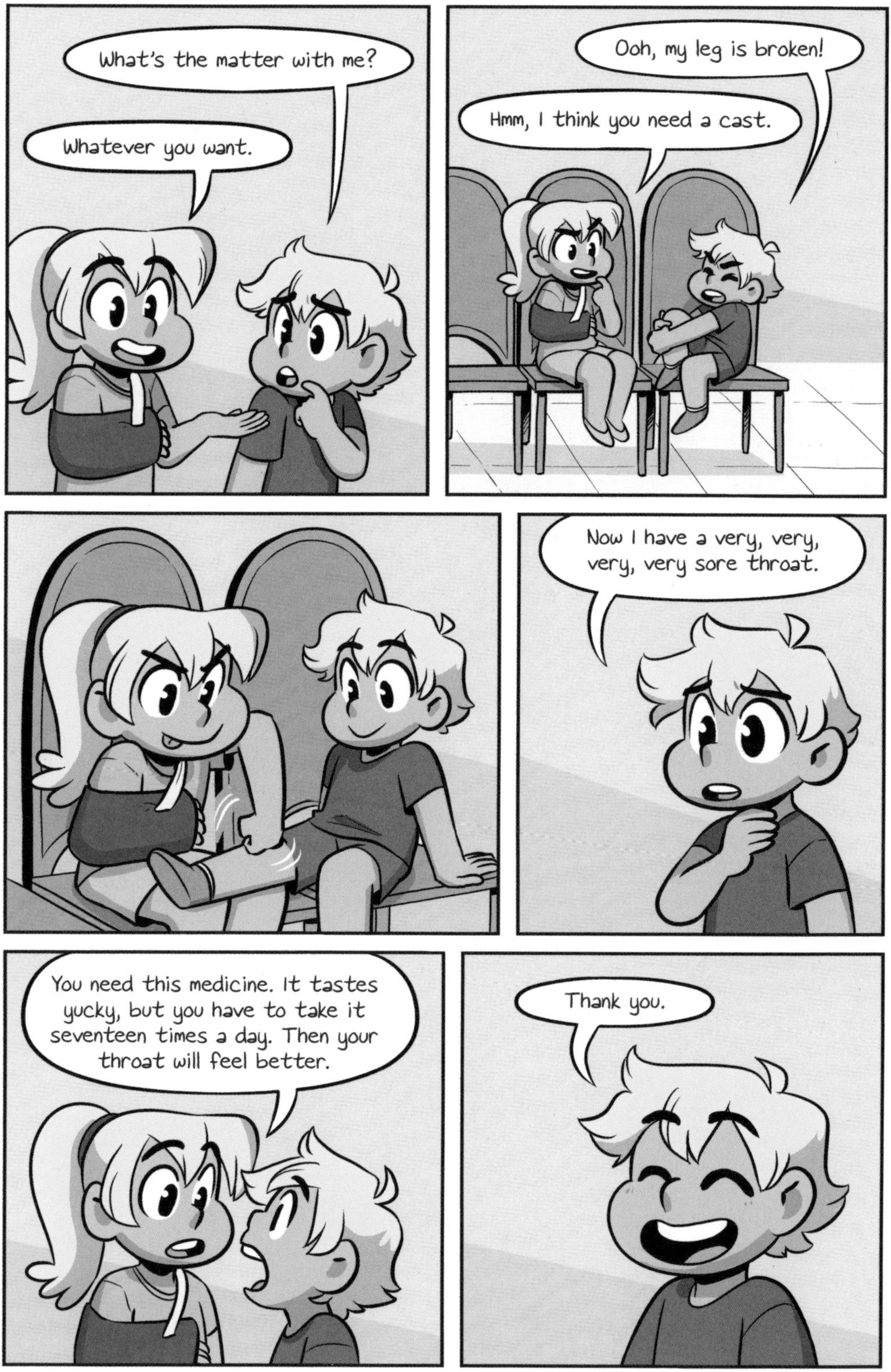
What's the matter with me?
Whatever you want.
Ooh, my leg is broken!
Hmm, I think you need a cast.
Now I have a very, very, very, very sore throat.
You need this medicine. It tastes yucky, but you have to take it seventeen times a day. Then your throat will feel better.
Thank you.

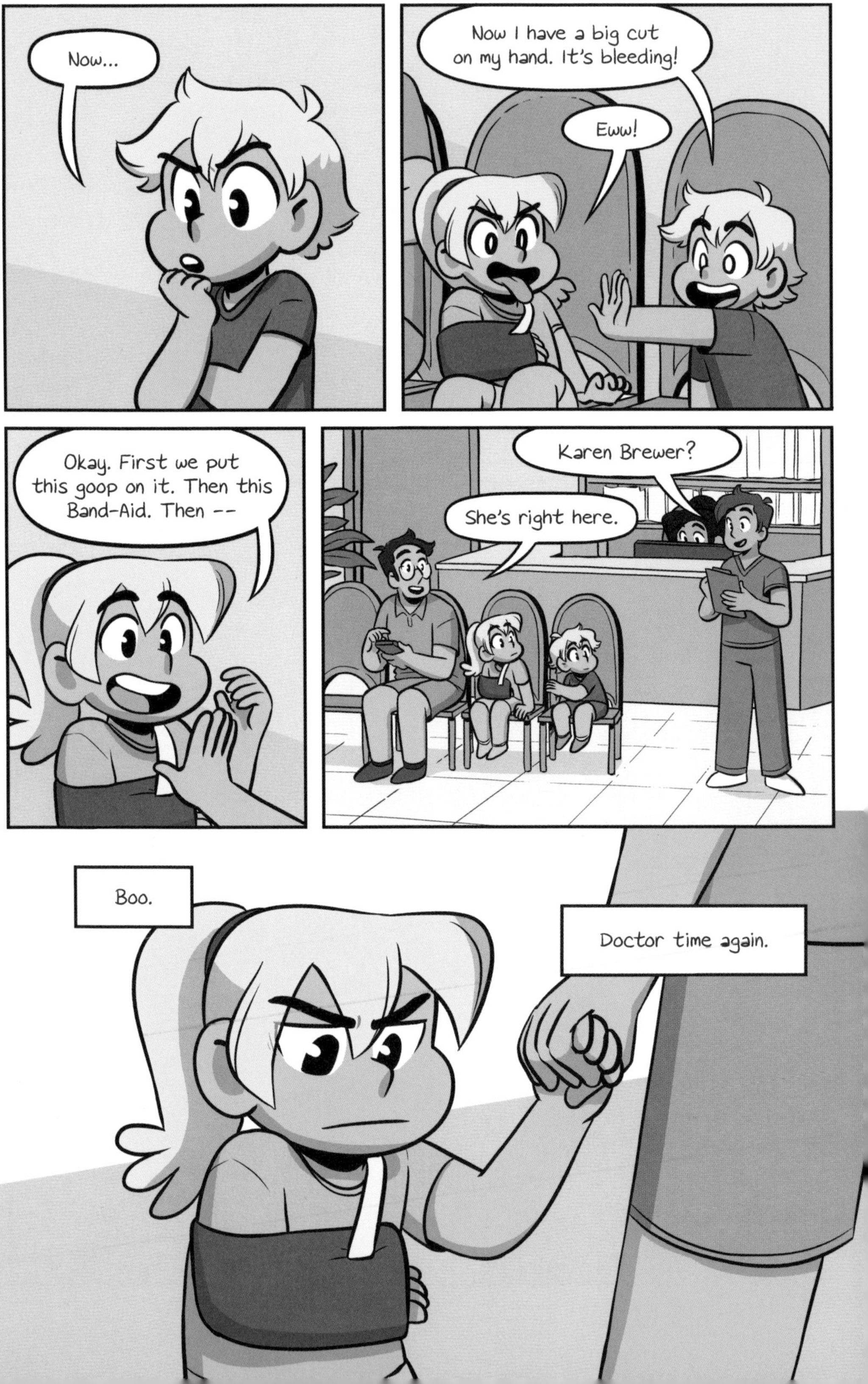
Now...
Now I have a big cut on my hand. It's bleeding!
Eww!
Okay. First we put this goop on it. Then this Band-Aid. Then --
Karen Brewer?
She's right here.
Boo.
Doctor time again.

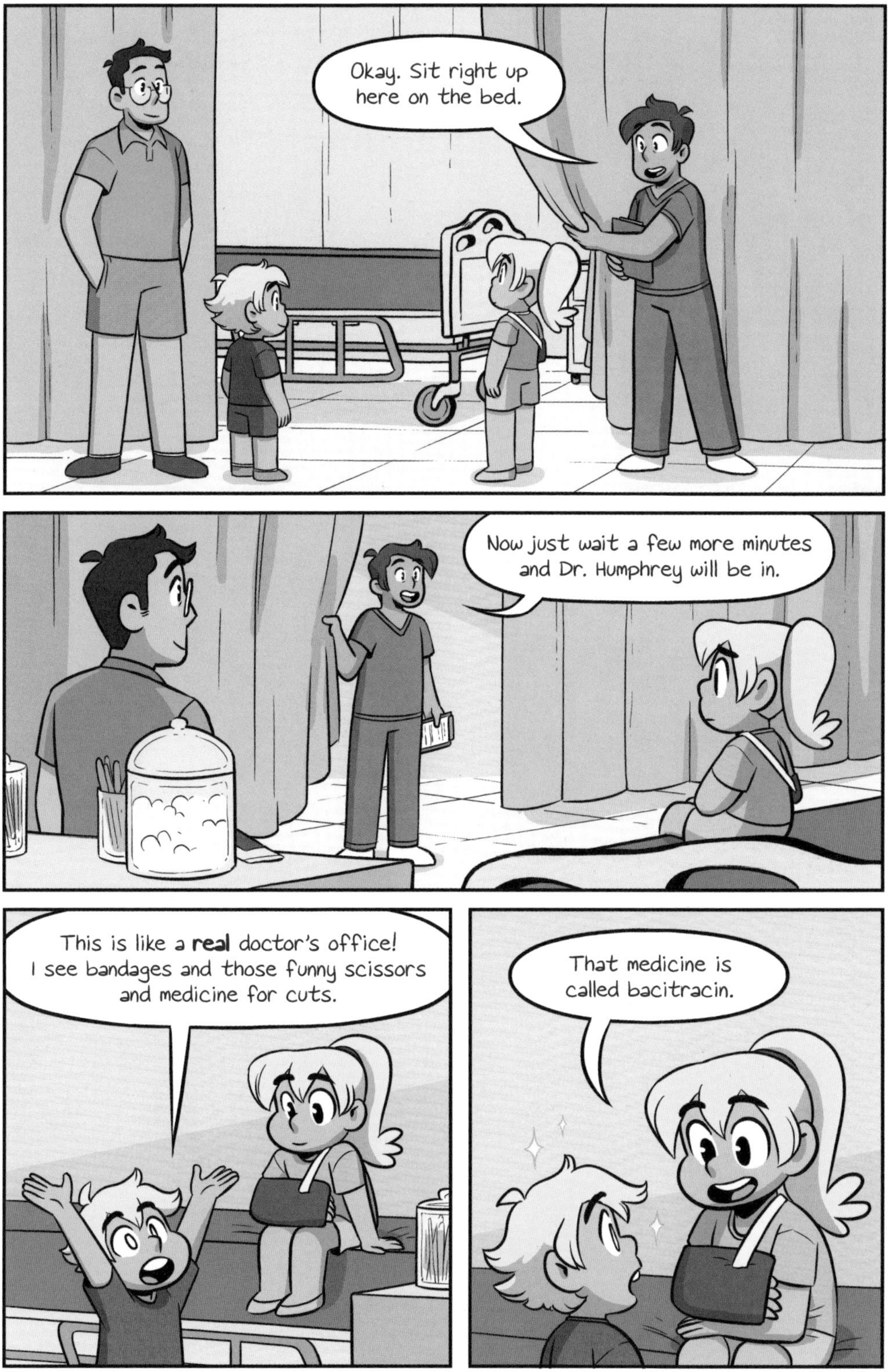
Okay. Sit right up here on the bed.
Now just wait a few more minutes and Dr. Humphrey will be in.
This is like a **real** doctor's office! I see bandages and those funny scissors and medicine for cuts.
That medicine is called bacitracin.

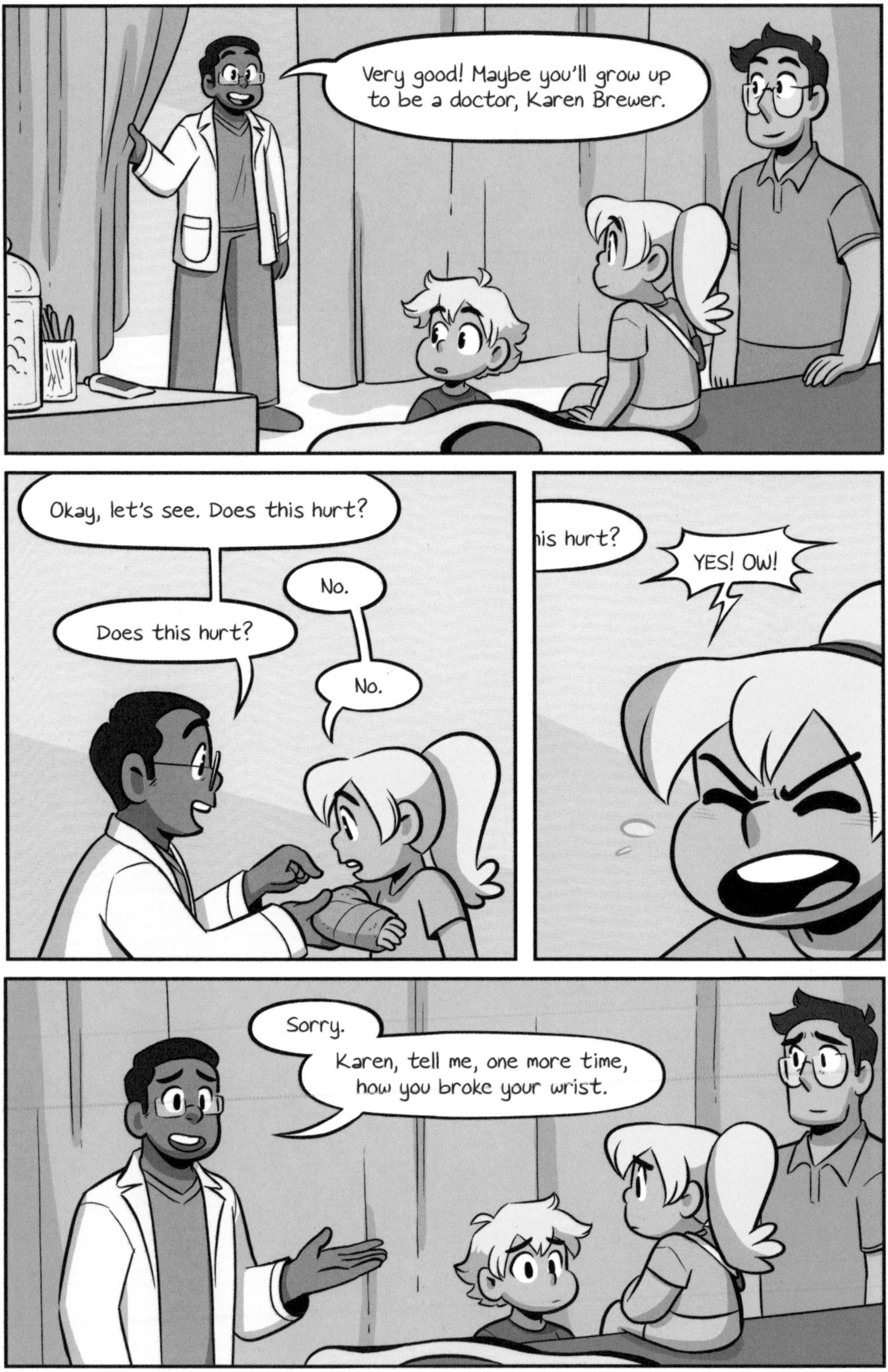
Very good! Maybe you'll grow up to be a doctor, Karen Brewer.
Okay, let's see. Does this hurt?
No.
Does this hurt?
No.
is hurt?
YES! OW!
Sorry.
Karen, tell me, one more time, how you broke your wrist.

CHAPTER 5

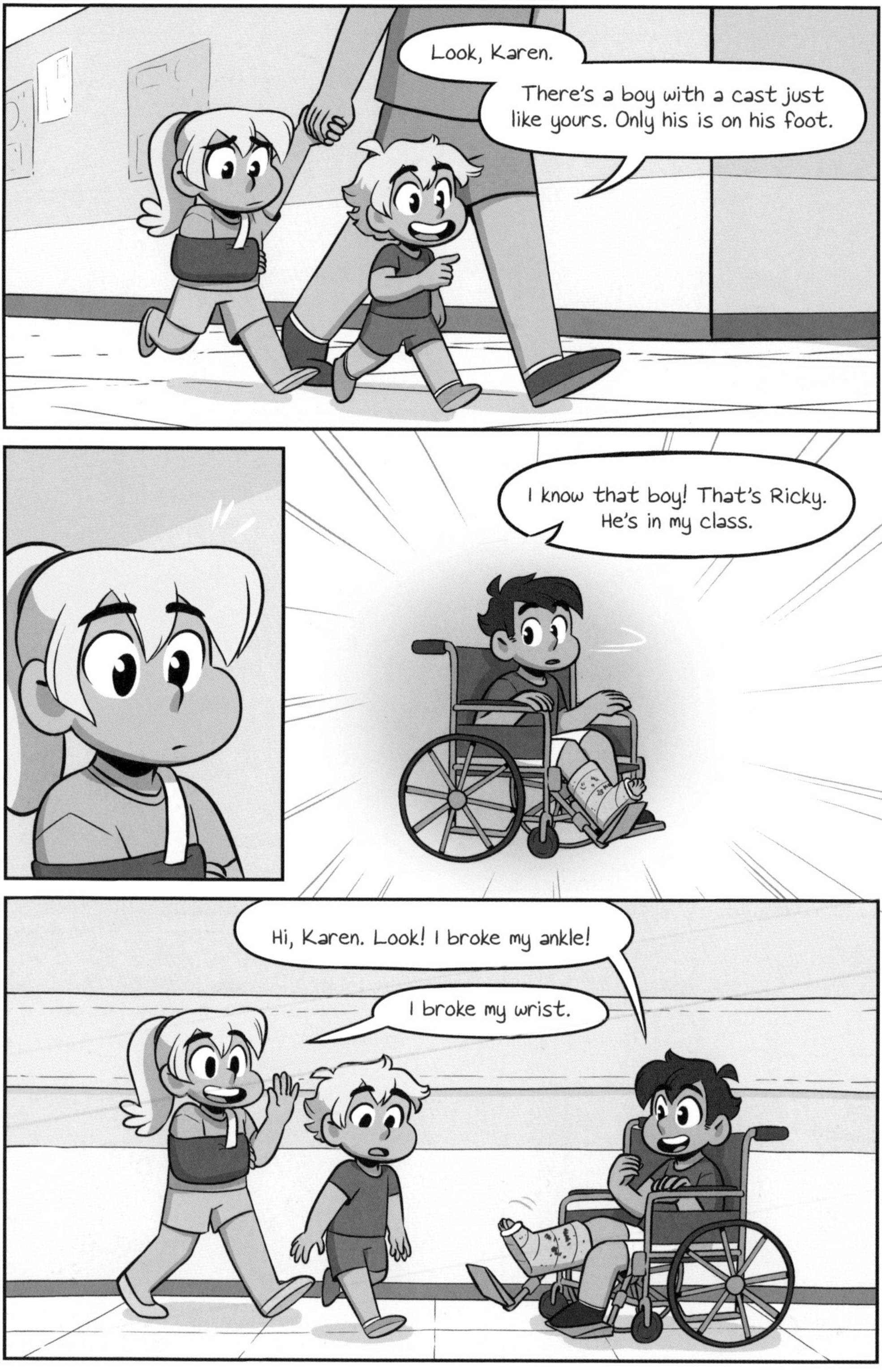
Look, Karen.
There's a boy with a cast just like yours. Only his is on his foot.
I know that boy! That's Ricky. He's in my class.
Hi, Karen. Look! I broke my ankle!
I broke my wrist.

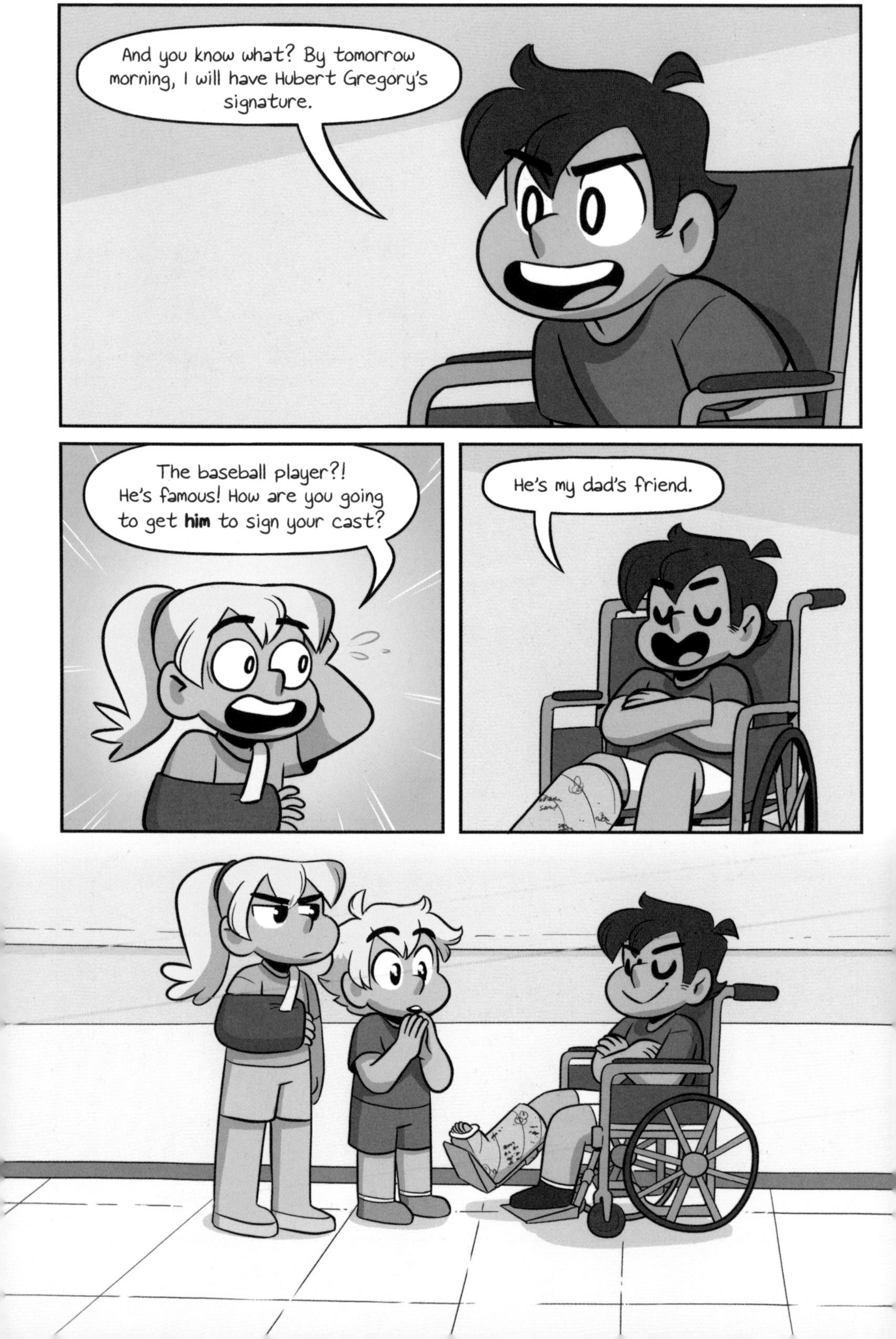
And you know what? By tomorrow morning, I will have Hubert Gregory's signature.
The baseball player?! He's famous! How are you going to get **him** to sign your cast?
He's my dad's friend.

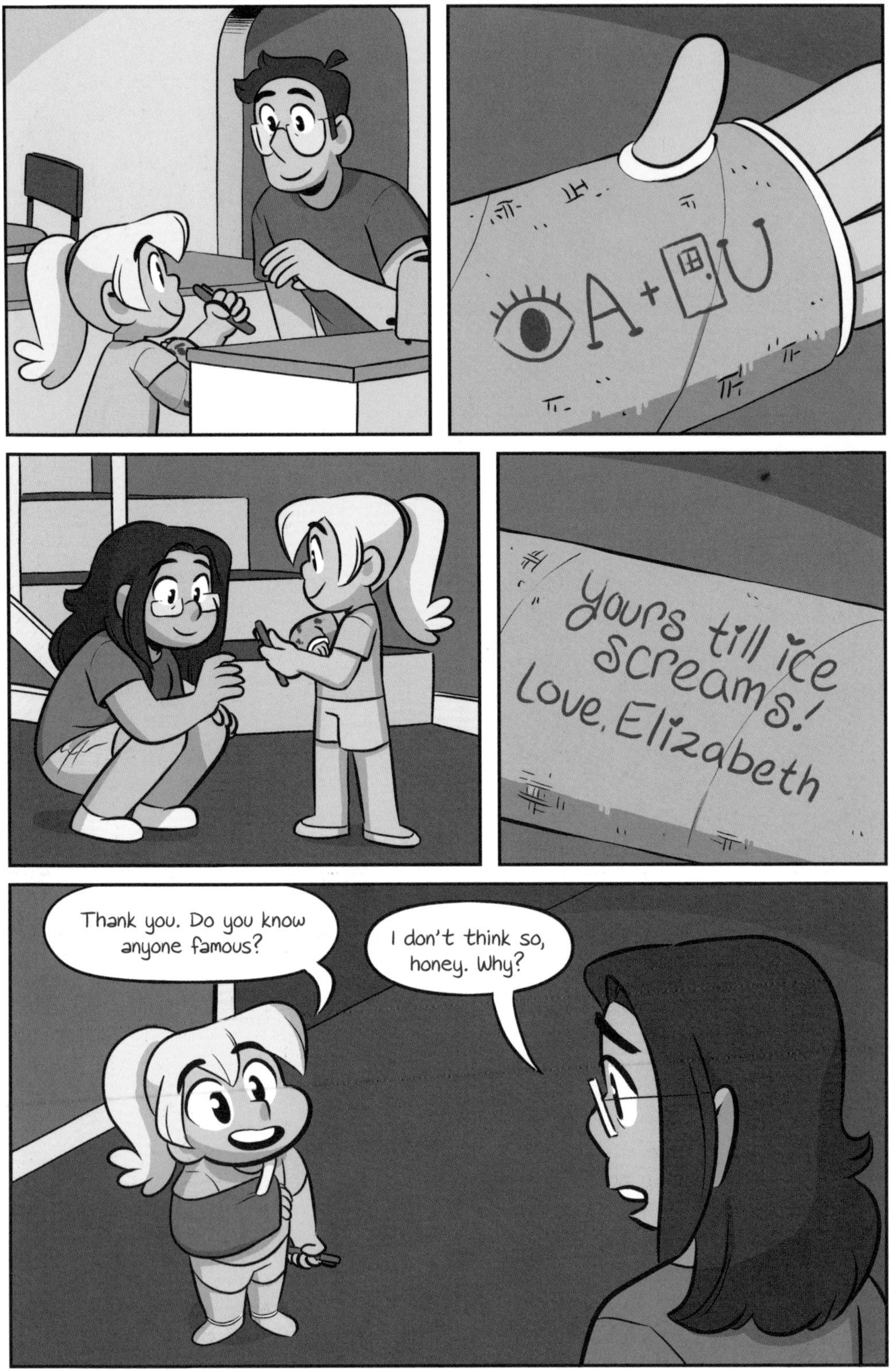

O A + [door] U
Yours till ice screams!
Love, Elizabeth
Thank you. Do you know anyone famous?
I don't think so, honey. Why?

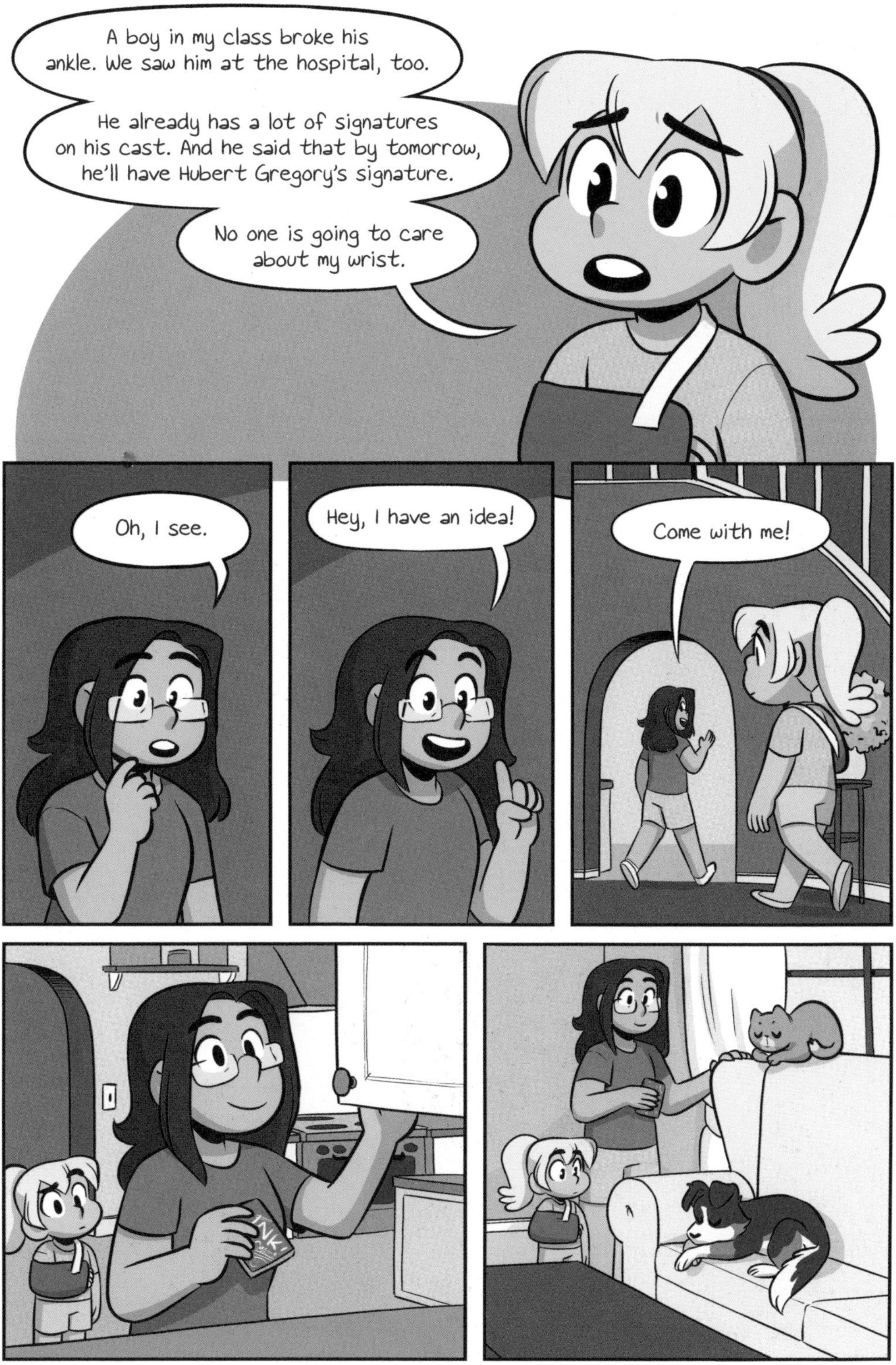

A boy in my class broke his ankle. We saw him at the hospital, too.
He already has a lot of signatures on his cast. And he said that by tomorrow, he'll have Hubert Gregory's signature.
No one is going to care about my wrist.
Oh, I see.
Hey, I have an idea!
Come with me!
INK!

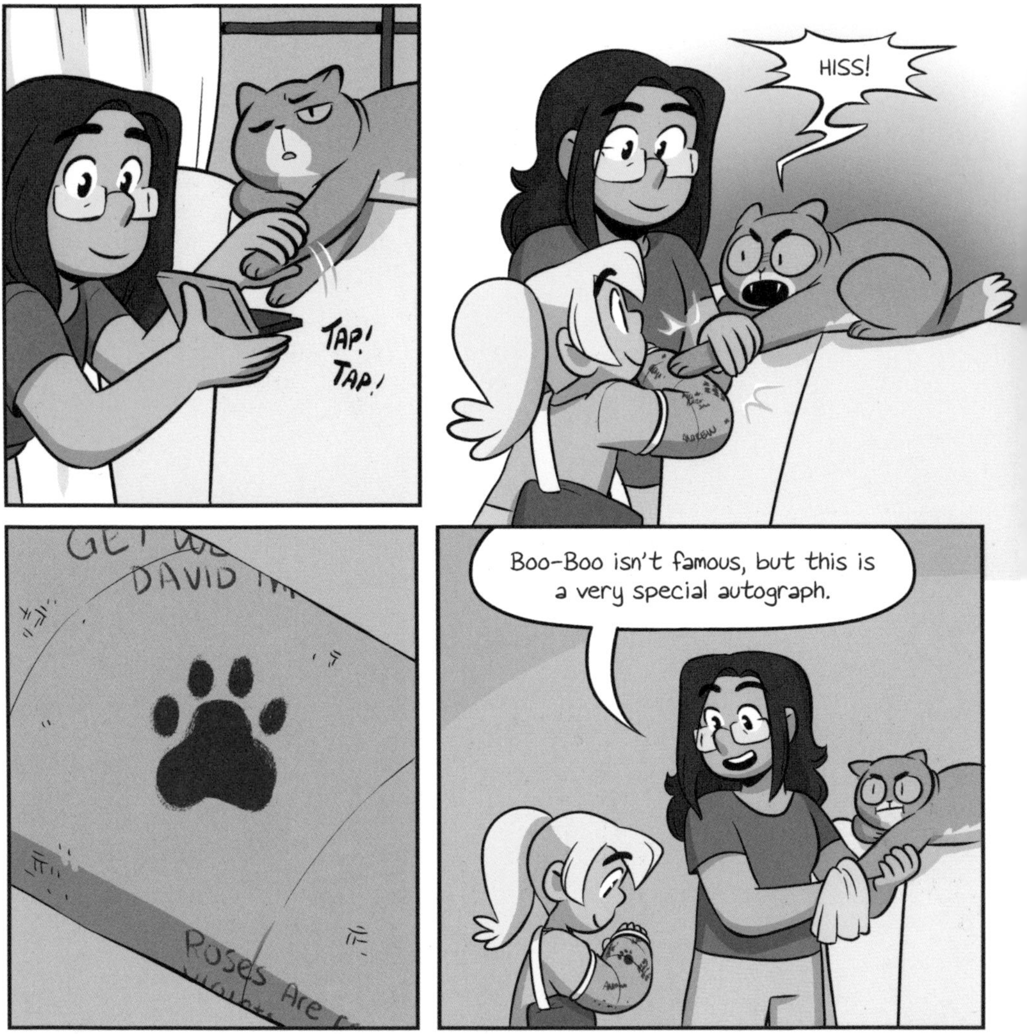
TAP! TAP!
HISS!
Boo-Boo isn't famous, but this is a very special autograph.
ANDREW

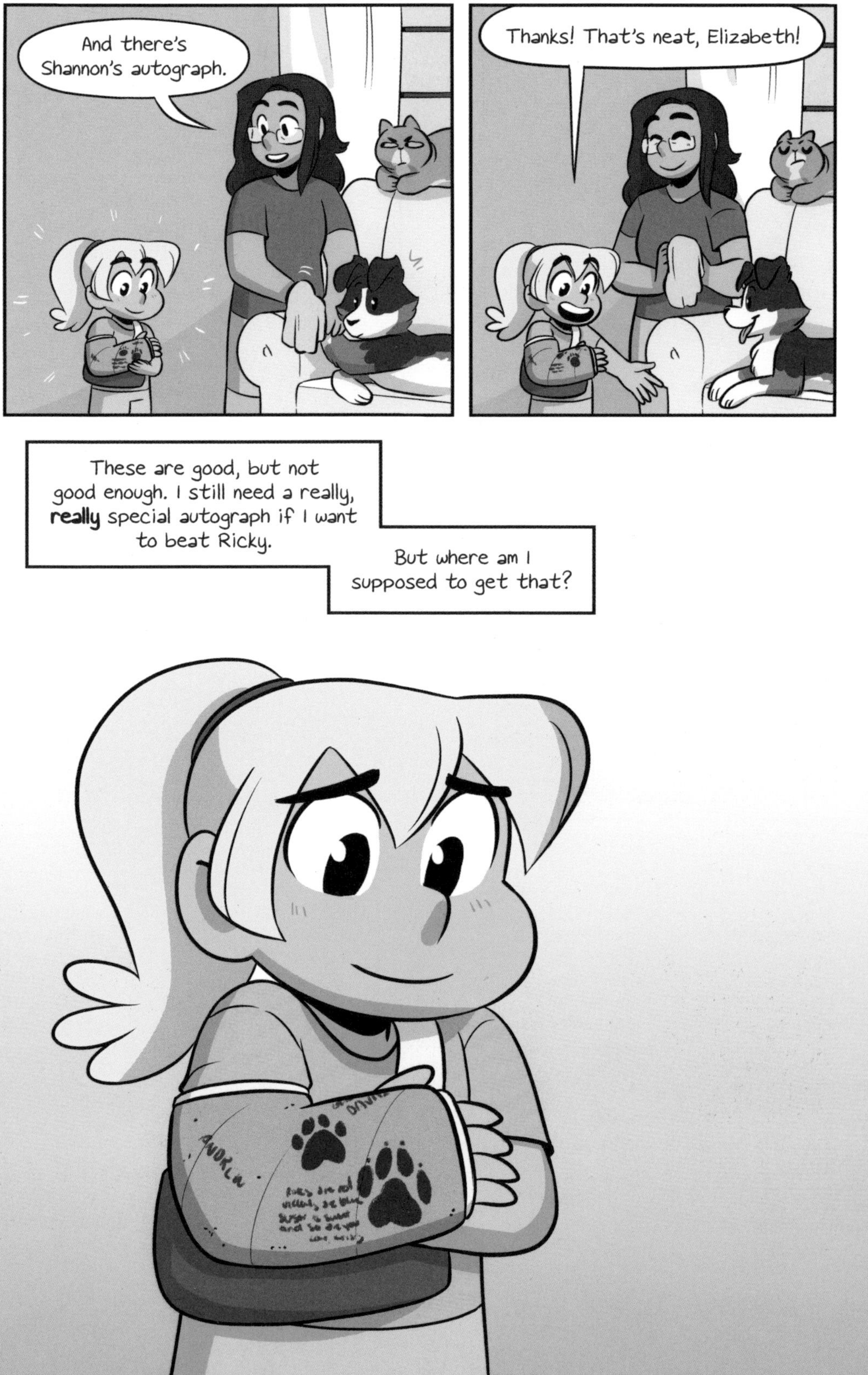

And there's Shannon's autograph.
Thanks! That's neat, Elizabeth!
These are good, but not good enough. I still need a really, **really** special autograph if I want to beat Ricky.
But where am I supposed to get that?

CHAPTER 6

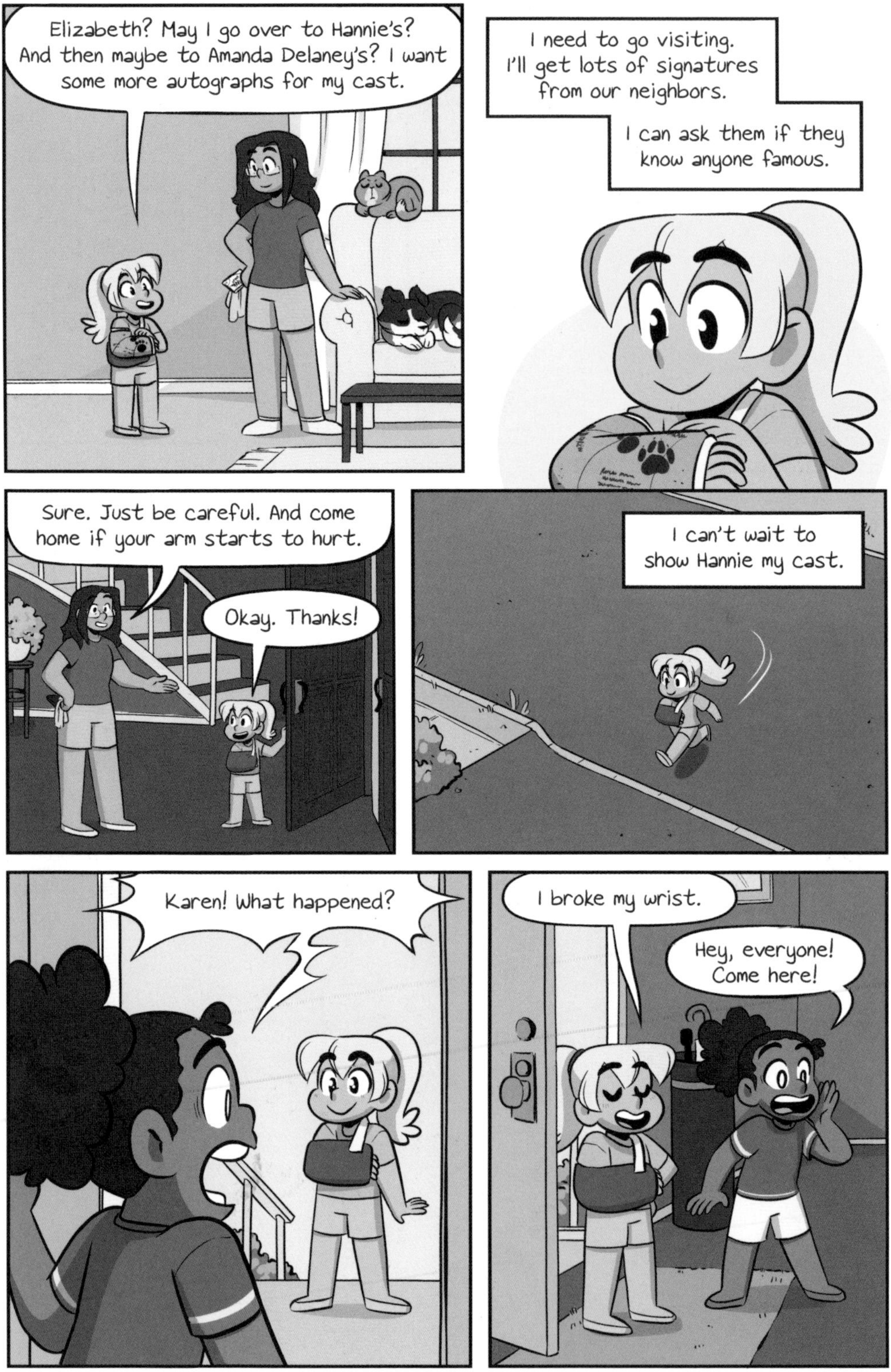
Elizabeth? May I go over to Hannie's? And then maybe to Amanda Delaney's? I want some more autographs for my cast.
I need to go visiting. I'll get lots of signatures from our neighbors.
I can ask them if they know anyone famous.
Sure. Just be careful. And come home if your arm starts to hurt.
Okay. Thanks!
I can't wait to show Hannie my cast.
Karen! What happened?
I broke my wrist.
Hey, everyone! Come here!

79

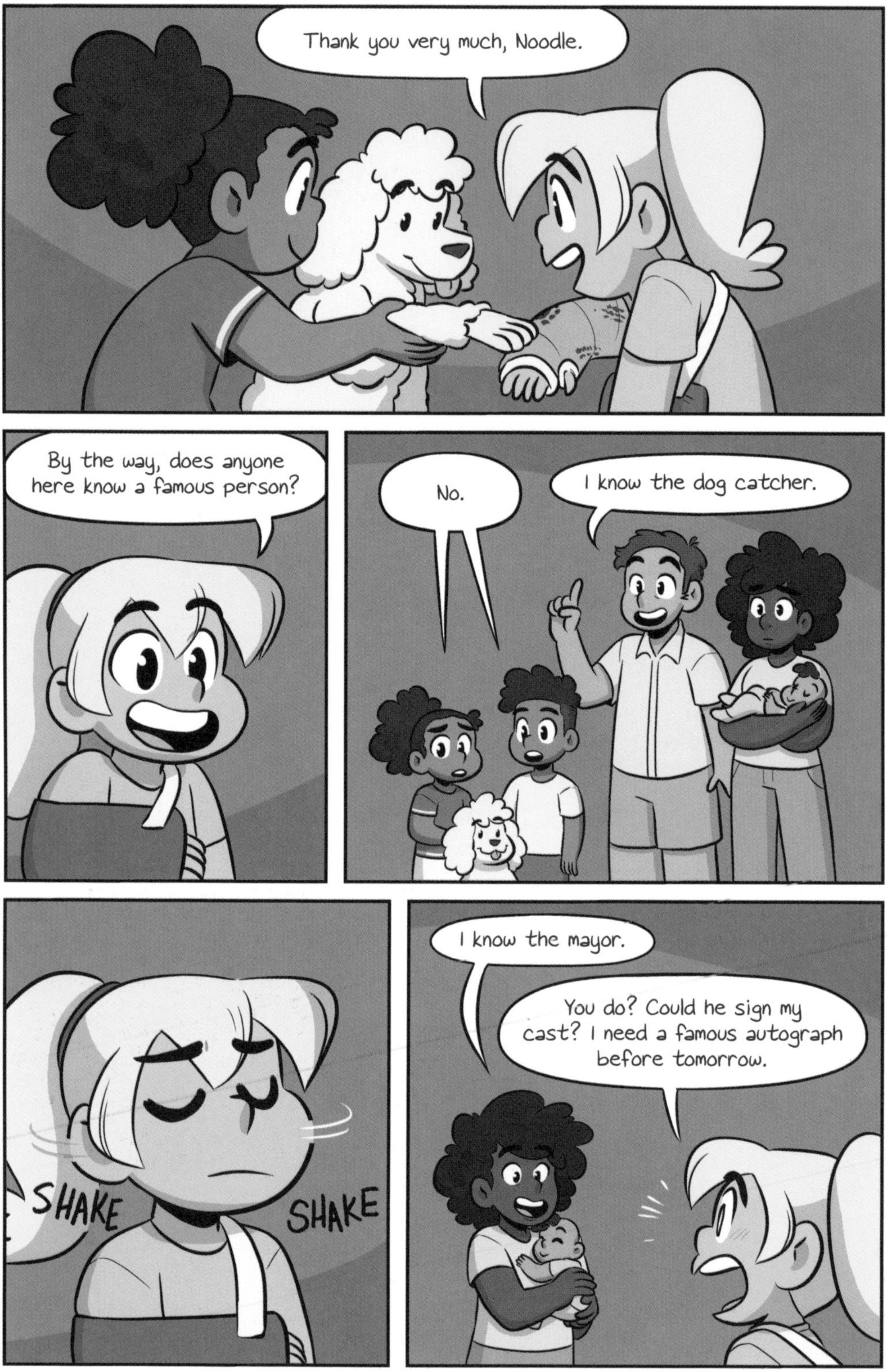
Thank you very much, Noodle.
By the way, does anyone here know a famous person?
No.
I know the dog catcher.
SHAKE
SHAKE
I know the mayor.
You do? Could he sign my cast? I need a famous autograph before tomorrow.

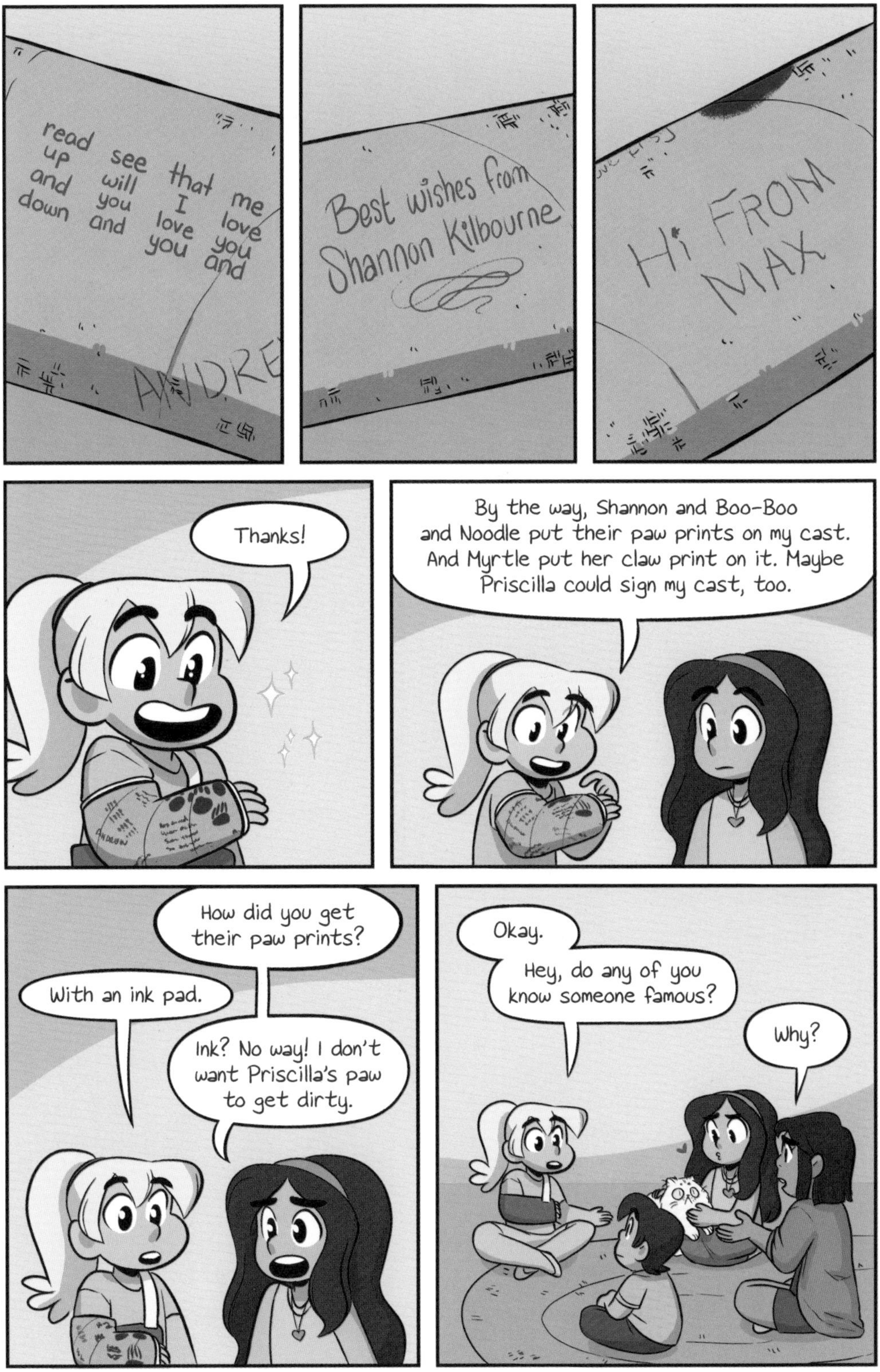
read up and down see will you and that I love you me love you and
ANDRE
Best wishes from Shannon Kilbourne
Hi FROM MAX
Thanks!
By the way, Shannon and Boo-Boo and Noodle put their paw prints on my cast. And Myrtle put her claw print on it. Maybe Priscilla could sign my cast, too.
How did you get their paw prints?
With an ink pad.
Ink? No way! I don't want Priscilla's paw to get dirty.
Okay.
Hey, do any of you know someone famous?
Why?

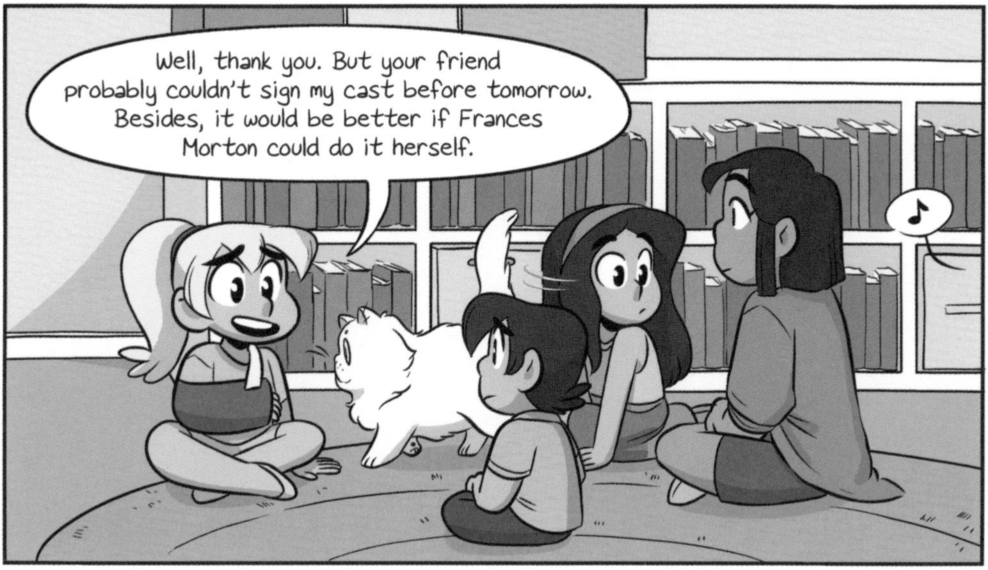
Well, thank you. But your friend probably couldn't sign my cast before tomorrow. Besides, it would be better if Frances Morton could do it herself.

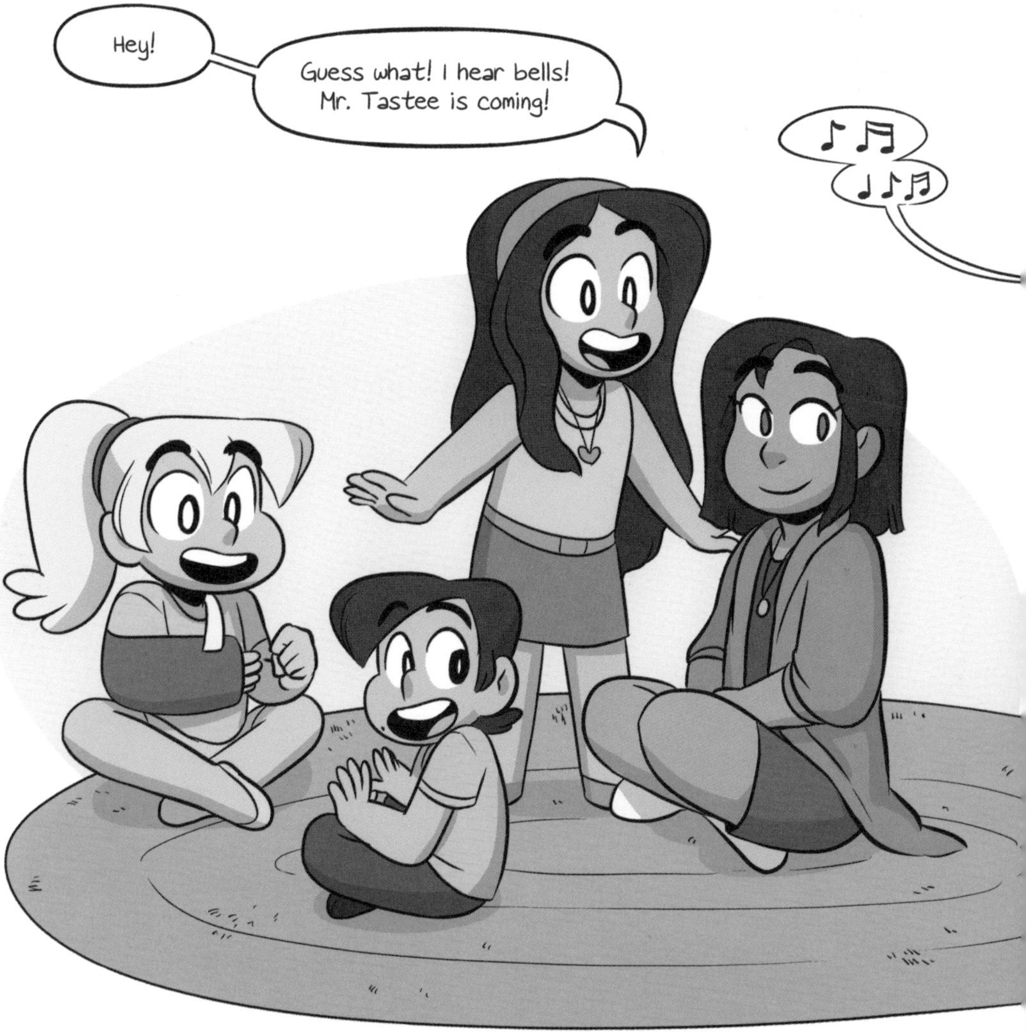
Hey!
Guess what! I hear bells! Mr. Tastee is coming!

CHAPTER 7

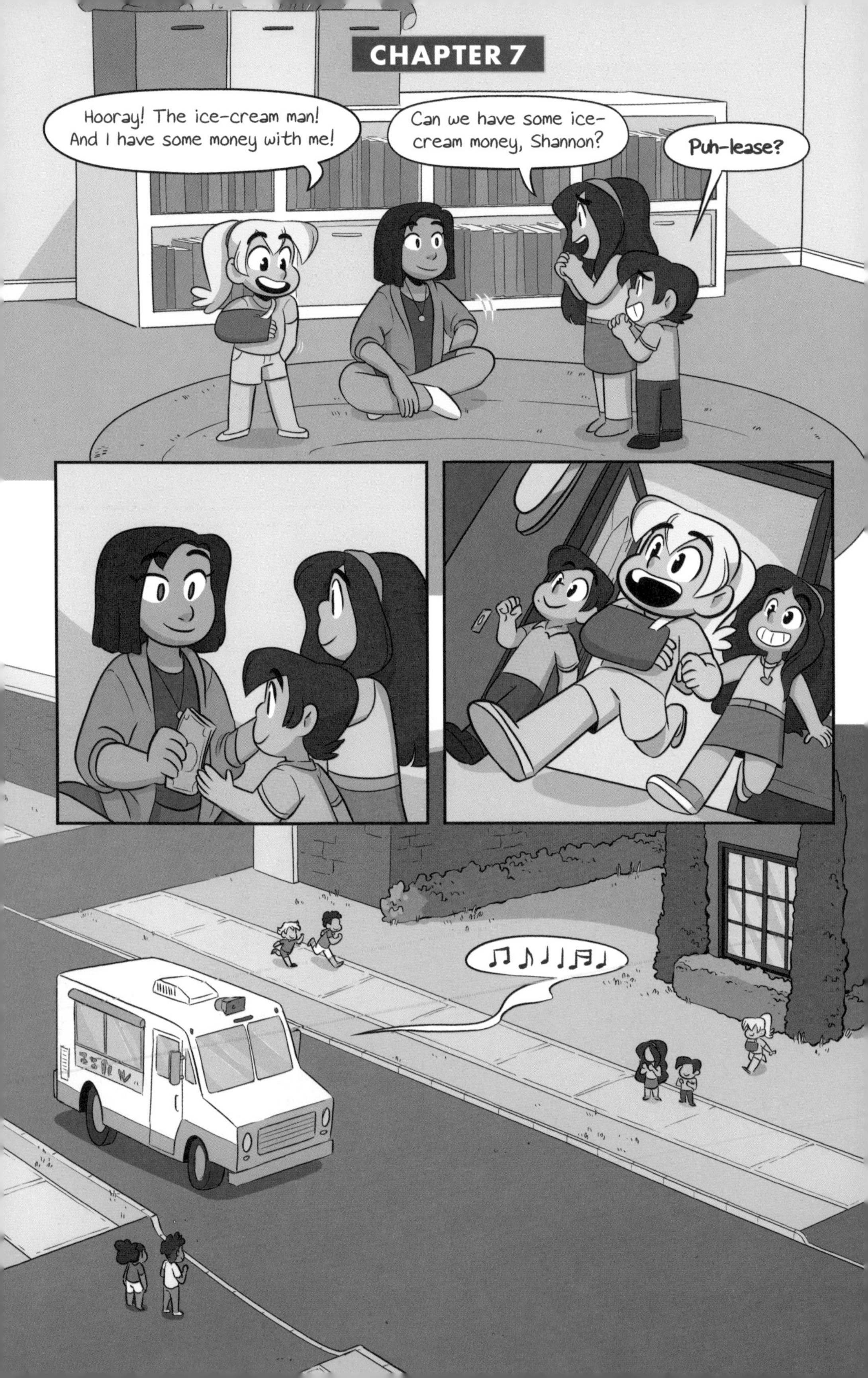
Hooray! The ice-cream man! And I have some money with me!
Can we have some ice-cream money, Shannon?
Puh-lease?

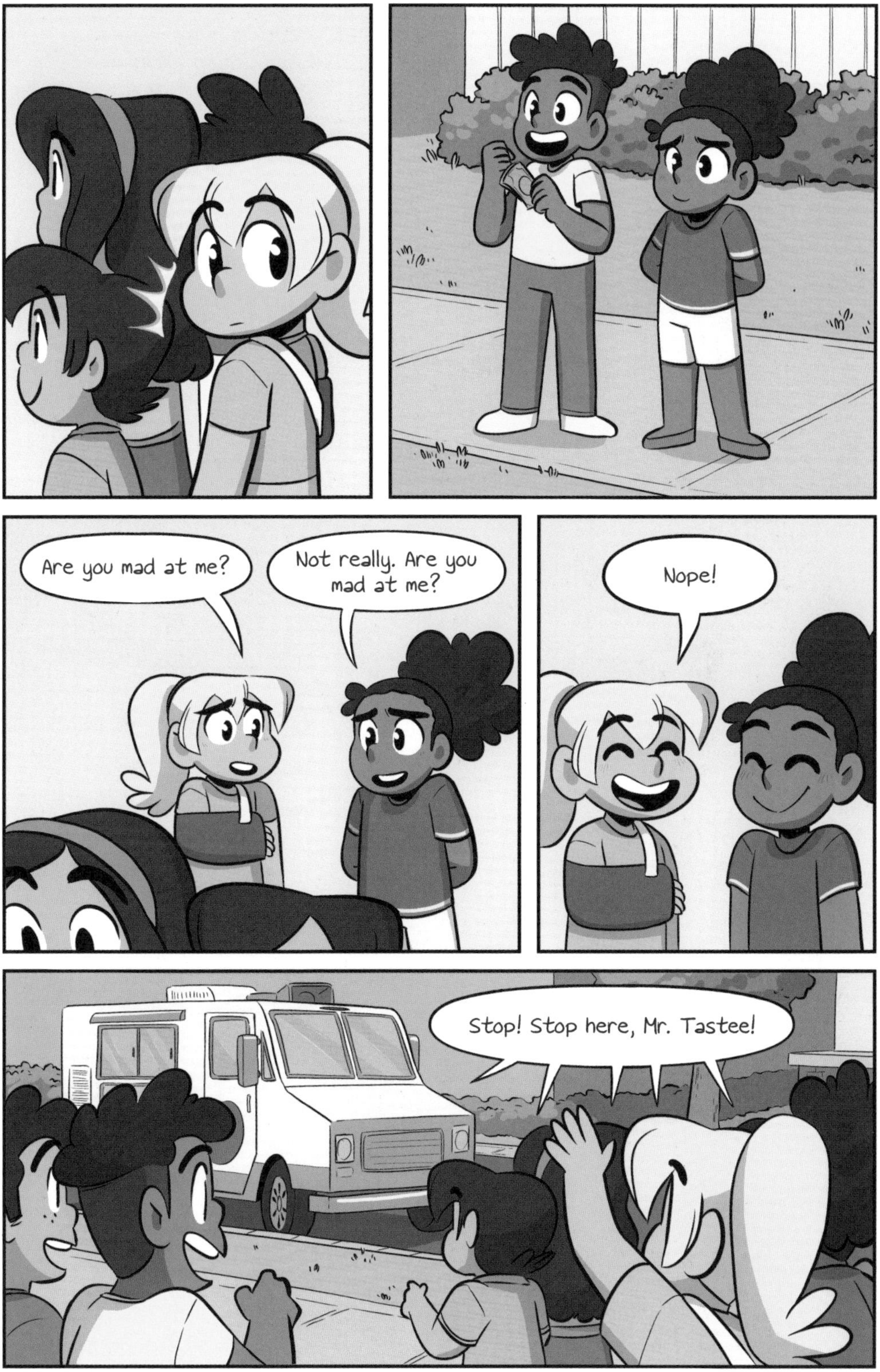
Are you mad at me?
Not really. Are you mad at me?
Nope!
Stop! Stop here, Mr. Tastee!

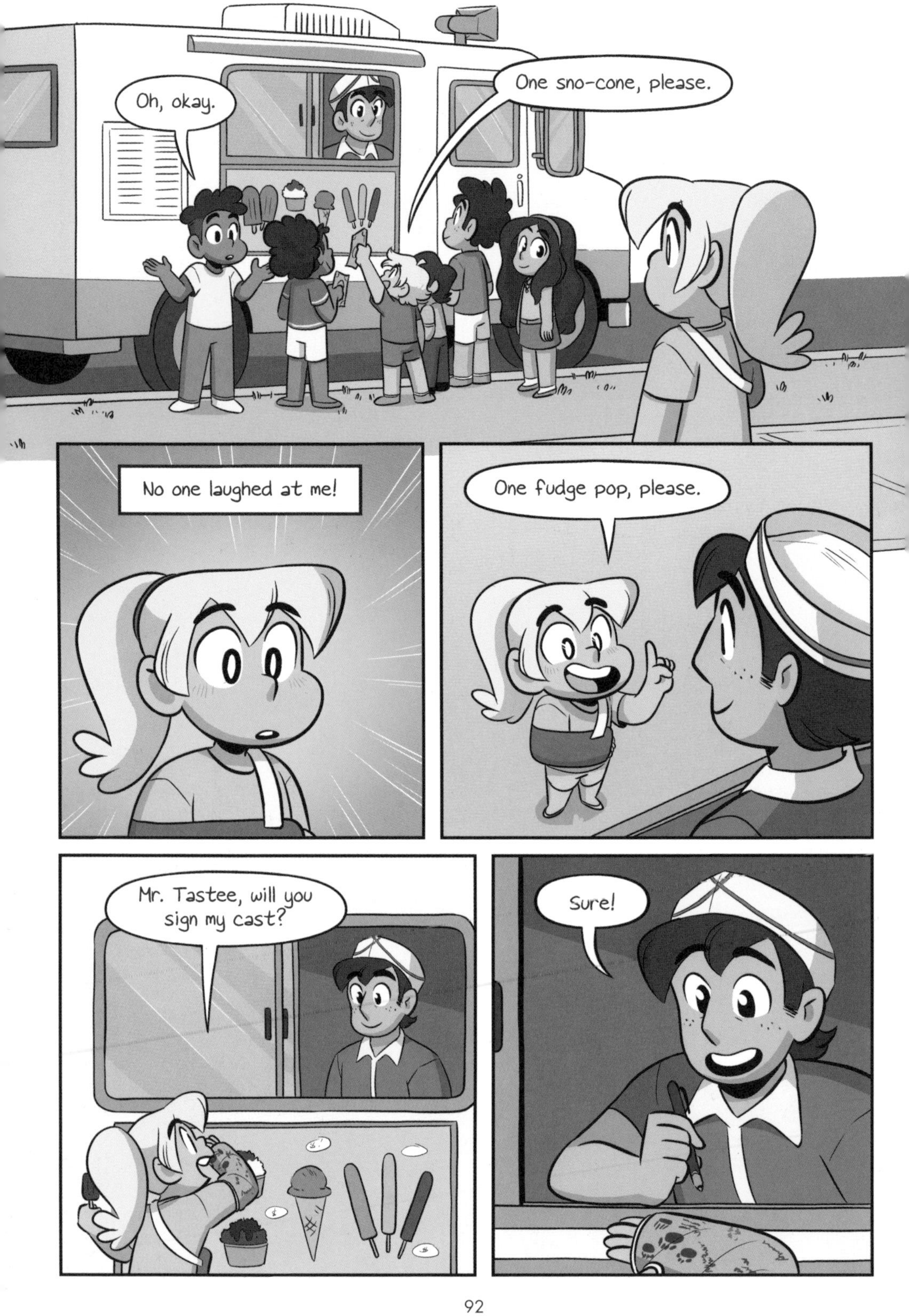
Oh, okay.
One sno-cone, please.
No one laughed at me!
One fudge pop, please.
Mr. Tastee, will you sign my cast?
Sure!

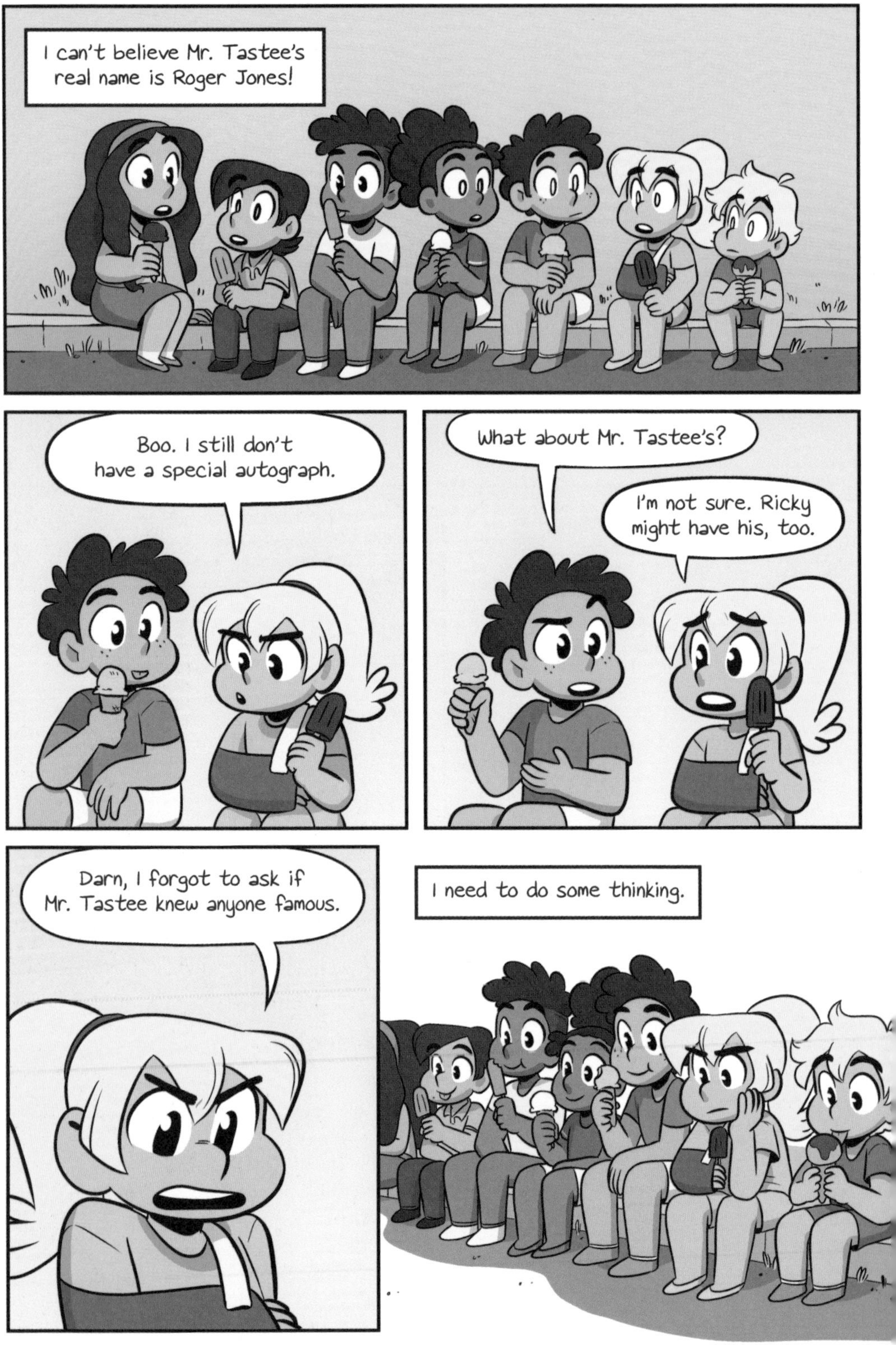
I can't believe Mr. Tastee's real name is Roger Jones!
Boo. I still don't have a special autograph.
What about Mr. Tastee's?
I'm not sure. Ricky might have his, too.
Darn, I forgot to ask if Mr. Tastee knew anyone famous.
I need to do some thinking.

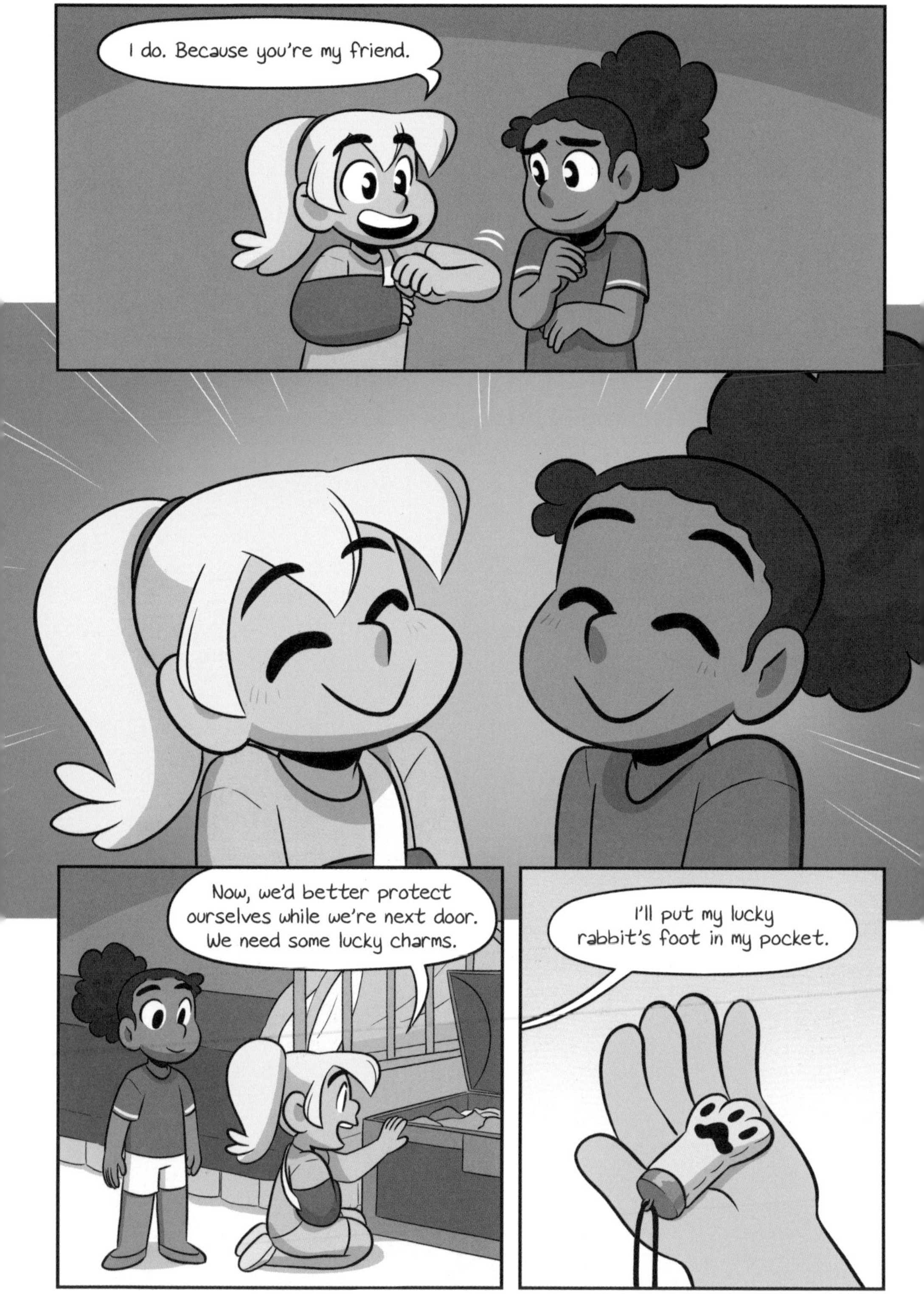
I do. Because you're my friend.
Now, we'd better protect ourselves while we're next door. We need some lucky charms.
I'll put my lucky rabbit's foot in my pocket.

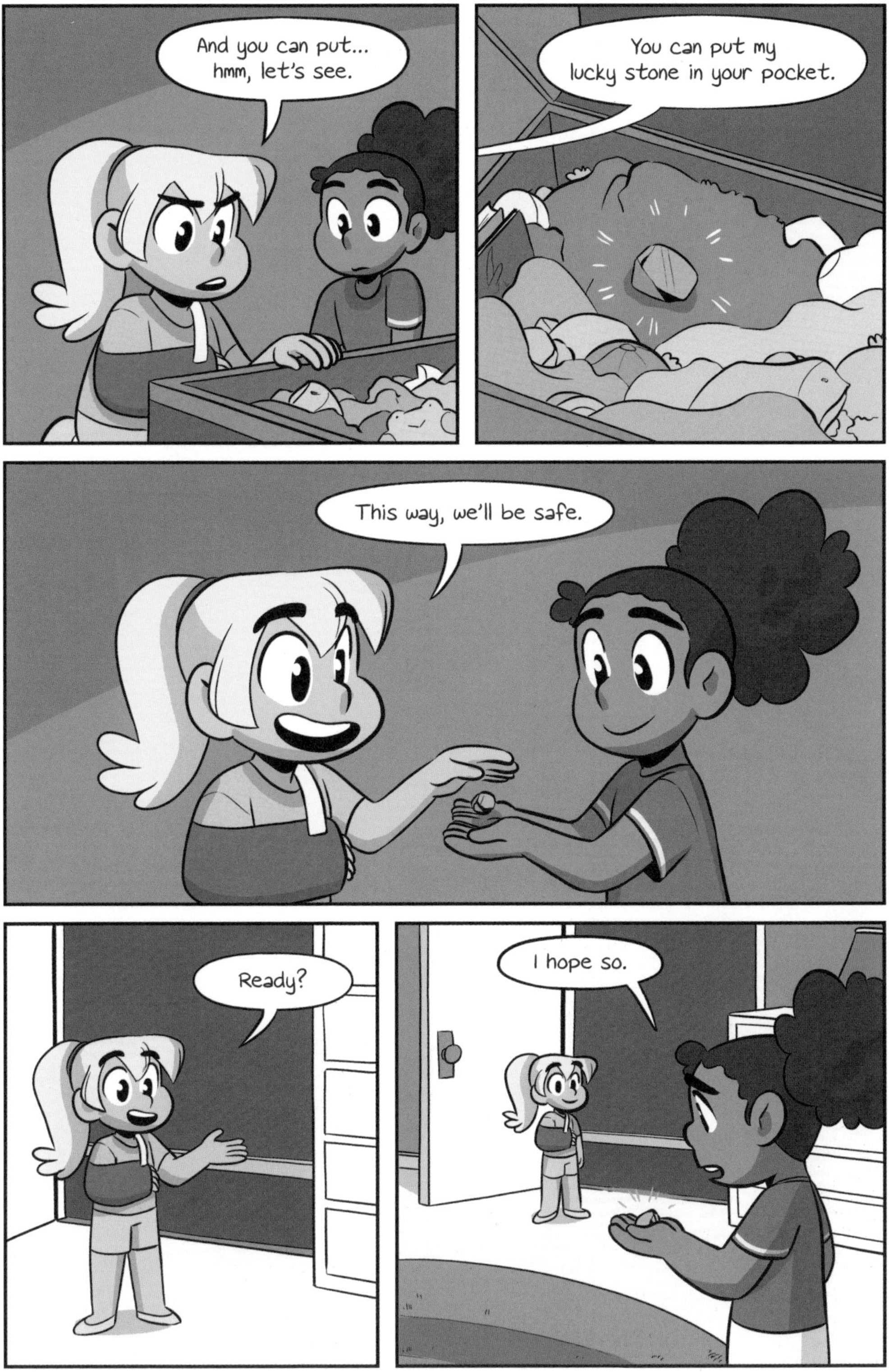
And you can put... hmm, let's see.
You can put my lucky stone in your pocket.
This way, we'll be safe.
Ready?
I hope so.

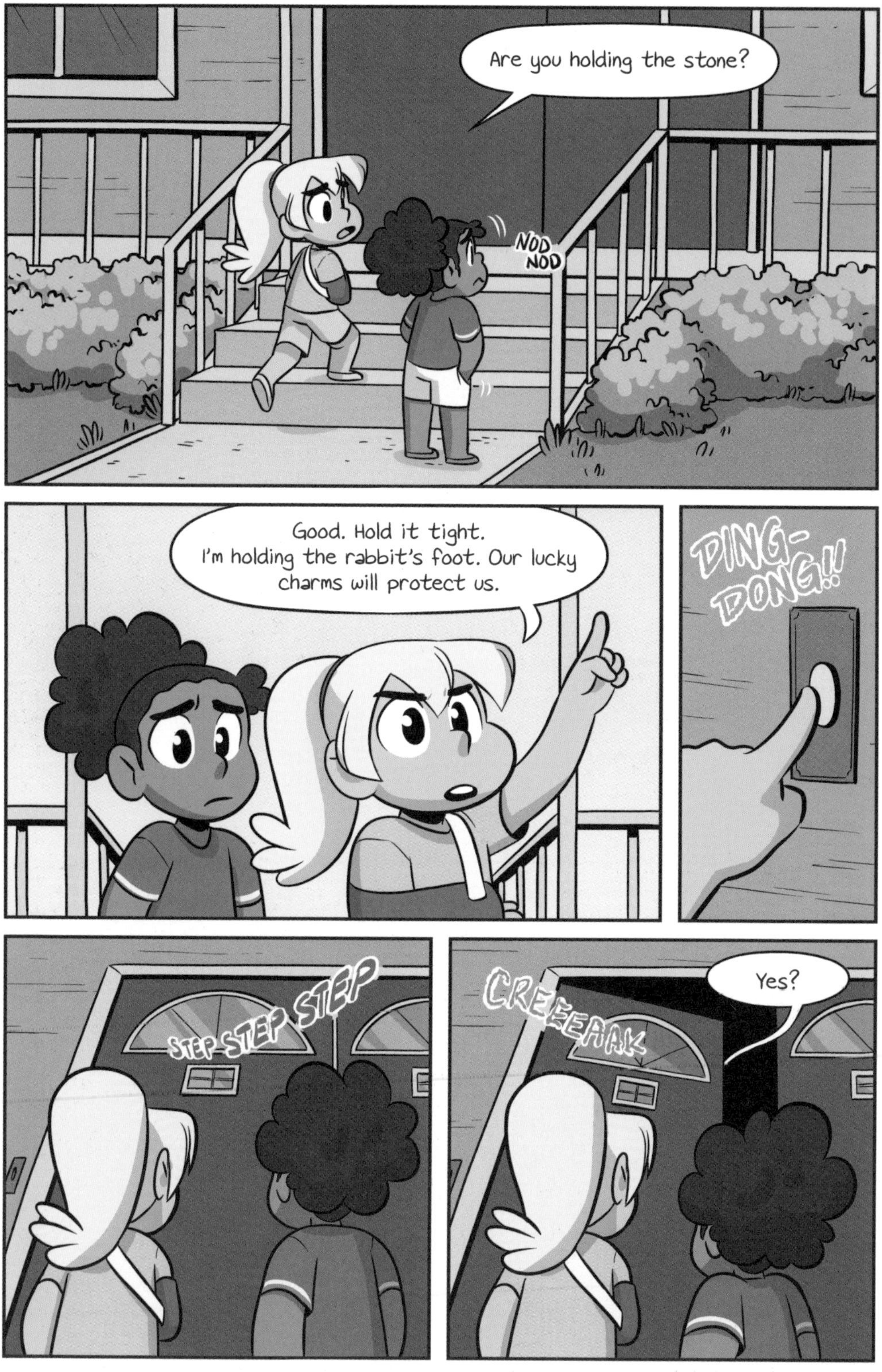
Are you holding the stone?
NOD NOD
Good. Hold it tight.
I'm holding the rabbit's foot. Our lucky charms will protect us.
DING-DONG!!
STEP STEP STEP
CREEEEAAK
Yes?

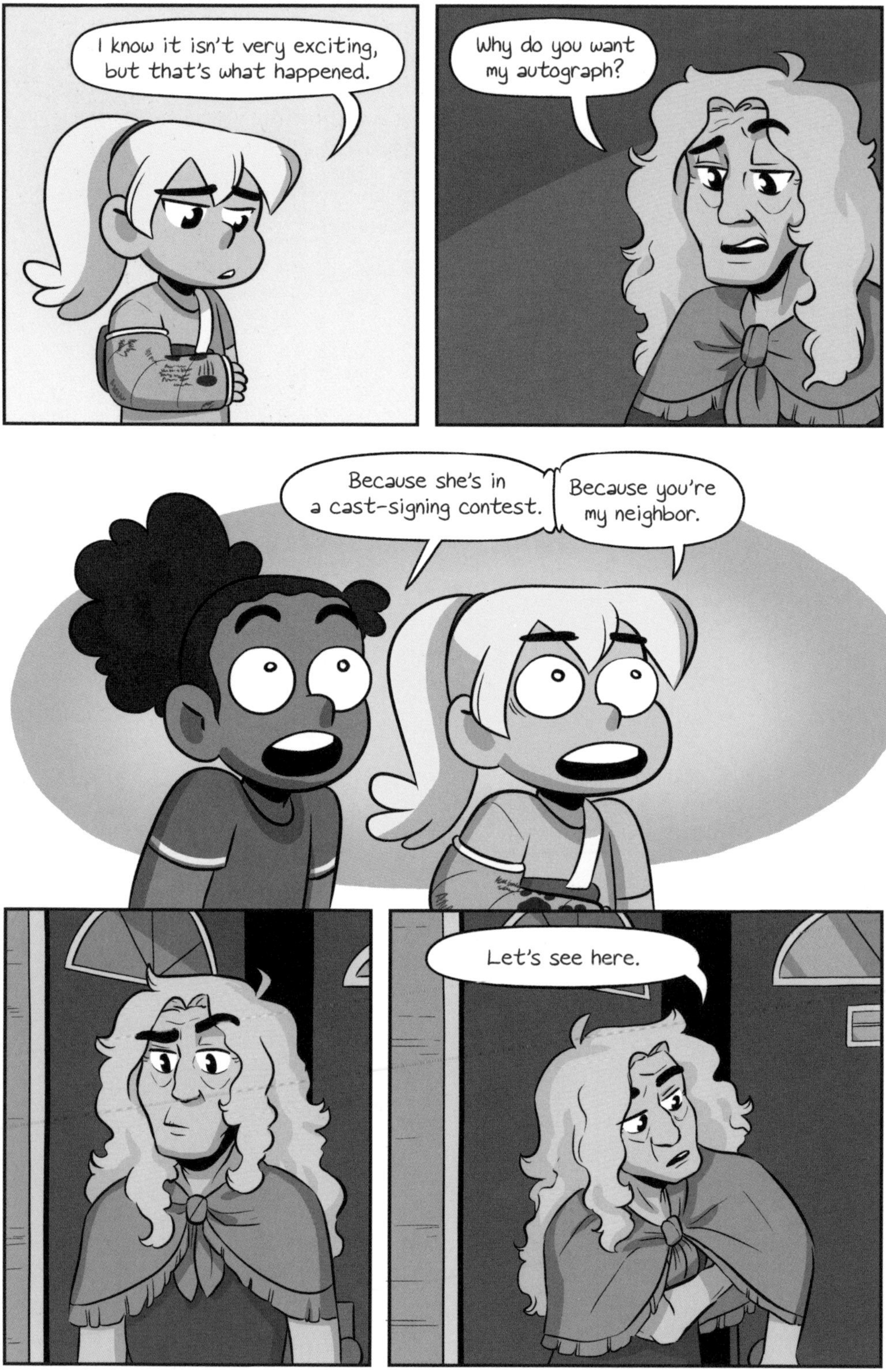
I know it isn't very exciting, but that's what happened.
Why do you want my autograph?
Because she's in a cast-signing contest.
Because you're my neighbor.
Let's see here.

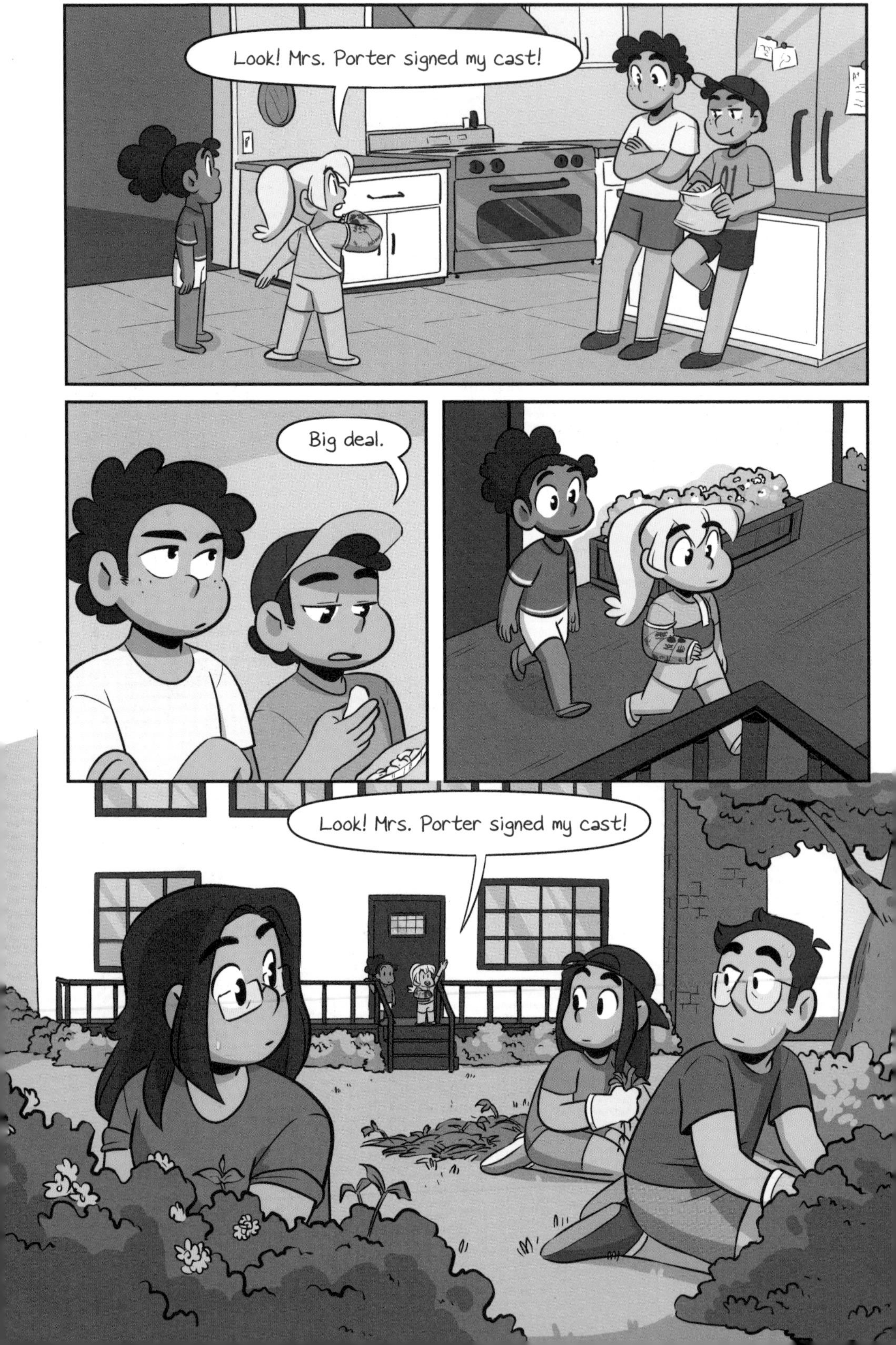
Look! Mrs. Porter signed my cast!
Big deal.
Look! Mrs. Porter signed my cast!

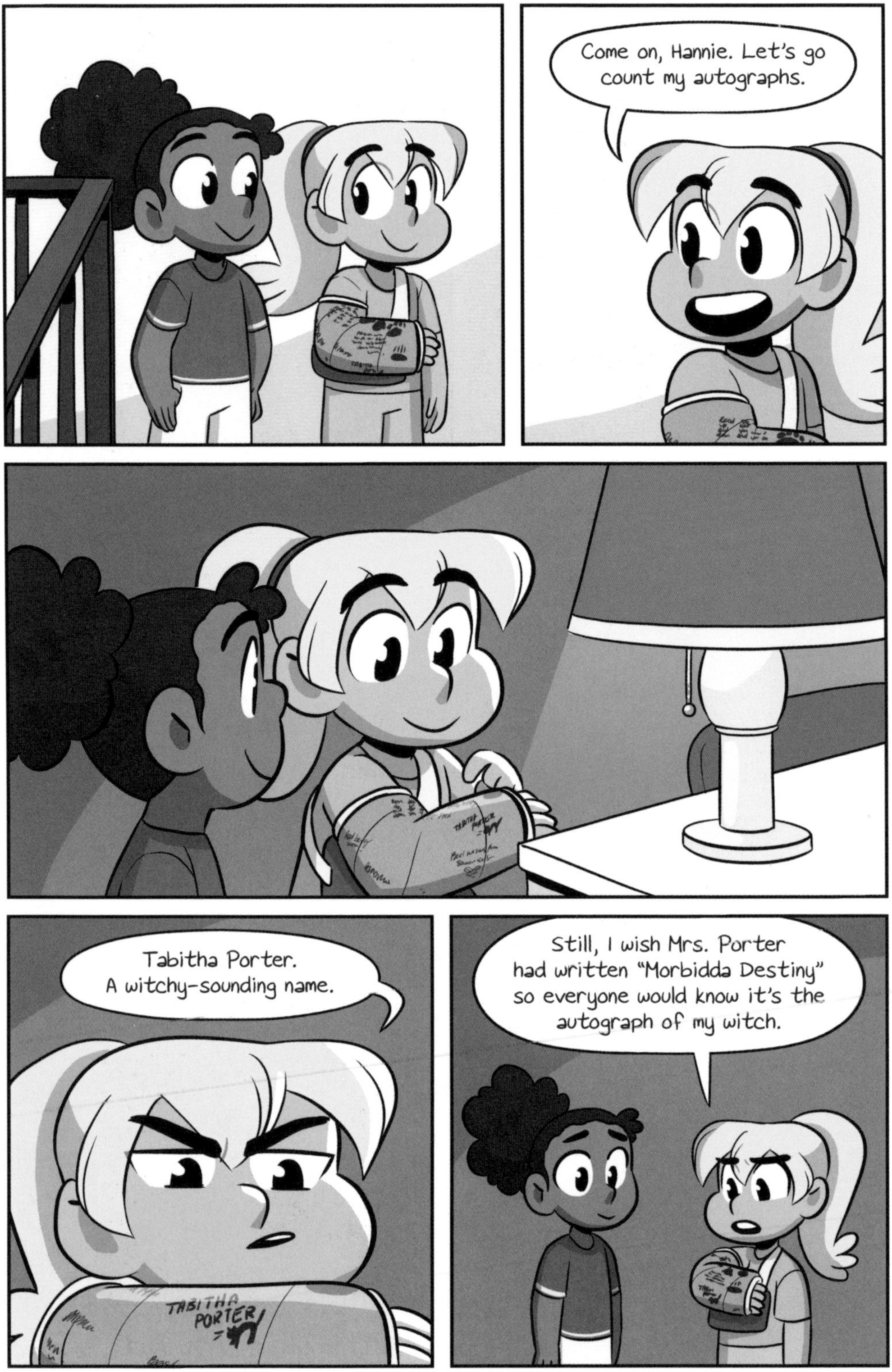
Come on, Hannie. Let's go count my autographs.
Tabitha Porter. A witchy-sounding name.
TABITHA PORTER
Still, I wish Mrs. Porter had written "Morbidda Destiny" so everyone would know it's the autograph of my witch.

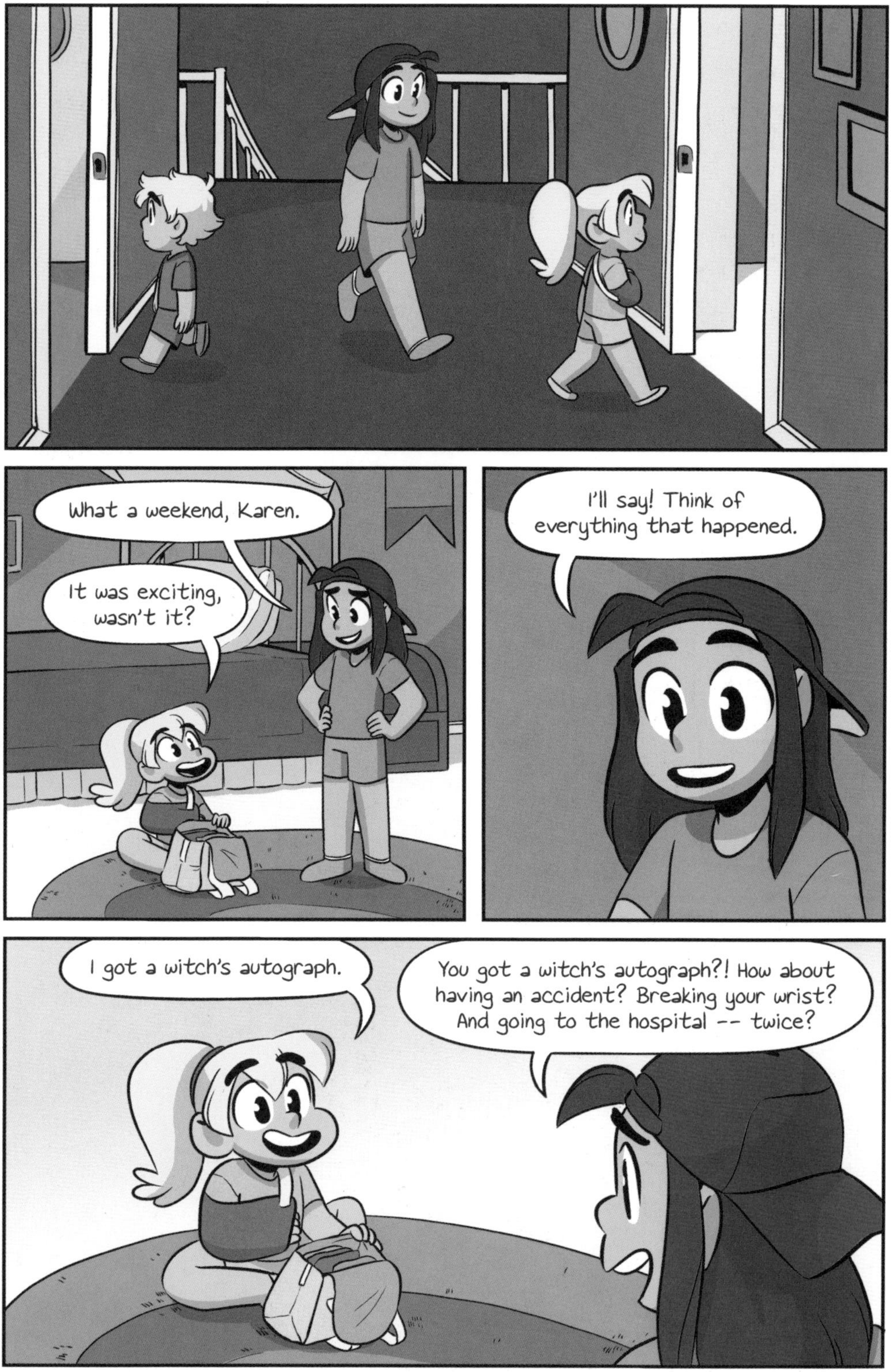

What a weekend, Karen.
It was exciting, wasn't it?
I'll say! Think of everything that happened.
I got a witch's autograph.
You got a witch's autograph?! How about having an accident? Breaking your wrist? And going to the hospital -- twice?

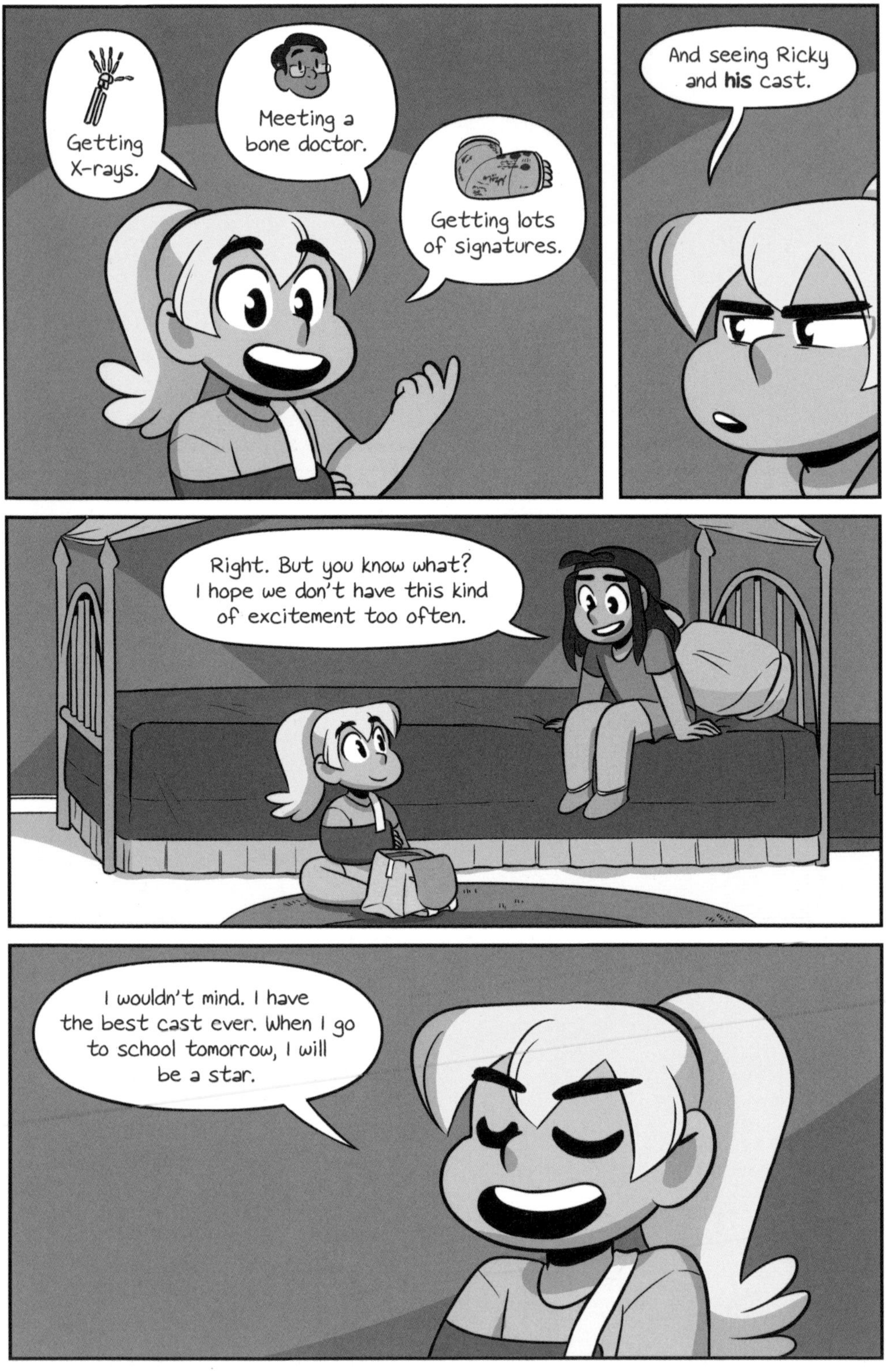
Getting X-rays.
Meeting a bone doctor.
Getting lots of signatures.
And seeing Ricky and **his** cast.
Right. But you know what? I hope we don't have this kind of excitement too often.
I wouldn't mind. I have the best cast ever. When I go to school tomorrow, I will be a star.